Frank L Webb

Questions and answers on the final examinations of the Law

Society for cerificate of fitness and call to the bar

Frank L Webb

Questions and answers on the final examinations of the Law Society for cerificate of fitness and call to the bar

ISBN/EAN: 9783741191909

Manufactured in Europe, USA, Canada, Australia, Japa

Cover: Foto ©Andreas Hilbeck / pixelio.de

Manufactured and distributed by brebook publishing software
(www.brebook.com)

Frank L Webb

Questions and answers on the final examinations of the Law

Society for cerificate of fitness and call to the bar

PREFACE.

The author's first motive was to supply himself with a complete collection of examination papers for his own use in preparing for the finals. Having done this the idea occurred to him that it would be important for all students to have such a collection, in order the more intelligently to make a practical application of the Principles of Law, as contained in the thirty thousand pages prescribed by the Law Society to be read for the final examinations. Accordingly he proceeded to write brief answers to the questions, and in almost all cases referred to the Text Books, Statutes or Rules from which the answer was taken, so that it might easily be supplemented by fuller information if the student should desire to read further in respect of it. The collection numbered over 800, and, after excluding the repetitions and those which were answered in "Roberts' Questions and Answers on Criminal Law," there remained about 500 questions, which, with the addition of the answers and the references, embody the main Principles of Law to be especially noted by the student. The student is recommended to read his Text Books carefully, and then a study of this work should be of valuable assistance to him in fixing and applying the Principles.

The author is indebted to Mr. D. C. Ross, Barrister, for a reading of the proof sheets while the work was passing through the press.

TABLE OF CONTENTS.

PART III.

TABLE OF REFERENCES.

Armour on Titles, (1887).

Taylor's Equity Jurisprudence, (1875).

Benjamin on Sales, American edition, (1888).

Smith's Mercantile Law, London Law Series, (1890).

Hawkins on Wills, (1872).

Smith on Contracts, (1885).

Blackstone, vol. I., (1869).

Pollock on Contracts, Blackstone Series, (1888).

Story's Equity Jurisprudence, (1886).

Theobald on Wills, (1881).

Harris' Criminal Law, (1881).

Broom's Common Law, (1888).

Dart's Vendors and Purchasers, (1876).

Best on Evidence, (1875).

Byles on Bills, (1885).

Leith's Blackstone, (1880).

Snell's Equity, (1887).

Taylor on Evidence, Blackstone Series, (1888),

Kingsford's Manual of Evidence, (1889).

Prideaux on Conveyancing, London Law Series, (1889).

Evans' Principal and Agent, Blackstone Series, (1888).

Wharton's Law Lexicon. London Law Series, (1889.)

Revised Statutes of Canada, (1886).

Revised Statutes of Ontario, (1887).

Consolidated Rules of Practice, (1888).

PART I.

CERTIFICATE OF FITNESS.

PART I.
CERTIFICATE OF FITNESS.

CHAPTER I.

REAL PROPERTY AND WILLS.

1. Q.—(1) A devise to a trustee in trust to pay the rents and profits to A. (2) A devise to a trustee in trust to permit A. to receive the rents and profits. (3) A de.ise to a trustee to pay rent or else permit A. to receive the rents and profits. In whom does the legal estate vest in each case ?

A.—(1) Legal estate is in trustee.
    (2) Legal estate is in A.
    (3) Legal estate is in A.

Hawkins, pp. 140 and 141.

2. Q.—A testator gives all his real and personal estate to *A. or his heirs.* How would this be construed as to the realty and personalty respectively ? Explain.

A.—If personal estate be given to *A. or his heirs*, the word " heirs " is read as a word not of limitation but of substitution, so as to prevent a lapse ; but in the case of real estate, if the substitutional construction were adopted, the result would be (in a will prior to 1838) to give to A. only an estate for life ; hence the rule as to real estate is different, viz.:—A devise of real estate to " A. *or* his heirs " gives to A. an estate in fee, the word " or " being read " and."

Hawkins, pp. 180 and 203.

3. Q.—A bequest to the children of A. to be divided between them equally when they attain 21 years. Some of the children die before 21 ; the others attain 21. How must the property be divided ?

A.—When there is a bequest of an aggregate fund to children as a class, and the *share* of *each* child is made payable on attaining a given age, or marriage, the period of distribution is the time when the first child becomes entitled to receive his share, and children coming into existence after that period are excluded.

Andrews v. *Partington, 3 Bro. C. C. 403.*

Hawkins, pp. 75, *et seq.*

4. Q.—Explain the doctrine of non-adverse possession. What is the present state of the law upon the subject ?

A.—The doctrine of non-adverse possession does not now apply except as to leases in writing at a rent of less than $4.00 per year. Formerly the possession of one might be consistent with the title of another, and to cause the Statute of Limitations to run it was necessary that there should be actual wrongful and tortious ouster ; but as for the law as it now exists, see

R. S. O. c. 111, s. 12.

5. Q.—A deed bears on its face an impossible date ; it is delivered as an escrow and subsequently delivered absolutely. What is the true date of the deed ?

A.—The true date is that of delivery.

Leith, p. 341.

6. Q.—What was and what is now the law respecting proof of purchase for value without notice. Can a purchaser of a mortgage set up that defence?

A.—See Armour on Titles, pp. 71-78.

7. Q.—What is the effect of imposing an impossible condition upon the grantees of an estate in fee simple?

A.—The condition will be void and the grantees will take the estate in fee.

8. Q.—At what period must notice of a prior conveyance be given to a subsequent purchaser who registers first in order to deprive him of the priority which he would otherwise gain over such prior conveyance by registration.

A.—Actual notice must be given before registration.

Armour, pp. 71 *et seq.*

9. Q.—A. dies intestate, leaving a wife and several children of full age. How does his estate, real and personal, descend?

A.—All property devolves on the Personal Representatives. The widow can take her dower, *i.e.* one-third interest in real estate for life, or she may elect to take against dower. The widow also has a right to one-third absolutely in the personalty. The children will be entitled equally, subject to the widow's dower, if she so elects, and her right to one-third of the personalty.

R. S. O. c. 108, s. 4.

10. Q.—What, if any, power has an executor (in the absence of a specific devise) or an administrator over the real estate of the deceased?

A.—See R. S. O. c. 108, ss. 8 and 9.

11. Q.—Within what time must a will be registered? What is the effect of non-registration?

A.—Twelve months from death of testator, or twelve months from the removal of any disability not caused by wilful neglect or default; but such disability must have existed from the death of the testator. Any person claiming title under an unregistered will is defeated by the prior registration of a conveyance from the heir, if it be *bona fide* and without notice.

> Armour, p. 214.
> R. S. O., c. 114, s. 76 and 77.

12. Q.—What is the present state of the law as to the right to set aside sales of reversionary interests?

A.—See Armour on Titles, pp. 258 *et seq.*

13. Q.—Define a precatory trust, and give examples of what are and what are not precatory trusts.

A. —The expression of a wish or desire on the part of the testator, accompanying a devise or bequest, that a particular application will be made of the property, is *prima facie* considered as obligatory, and creates a trust (called a precatory trust), unless an intention appear to the contrary. To create a precatory trust three *certainties* are necessary: (1) The words must be imperative. (2) The object certain. (3) The subject certain.

> Hawkins, pp. 159 *et seq.*

14. Q.—Give an example of a case in which " or " will be read as " and " in a will.

A.—*Fairfield* v. *Morgan, 2 B. & P. N. R. 38*, decides that if real estate be devised to A. in *fee simple* with limitation over in the event of A. dying under 21 or without issue, the word " or " will be read " and " and the gift over will be construed to take effect only in the event of A. dying under 21 and without issue.

Read v. *Snell, 2 Atk. 645*. This decision was based on the law as it existed before 1838, when a devise without words of limitation conferred merely a life estate, but to prevent a lapse the Court read a devise to A or his heirs as a devise to A. and his heirs, the word " or " being read " and."

15. Q.—A devise to A. for life and from and after his death to B. A devise to B. from and after his attaining the age of 20. What difference, if any, is there in the nature of B.'s interest under these two devises ?

A.—In the first case B. takes a vested estate in fee subject to the life estate of A., and in the second case B. has a contingent remainder—contingent on his attaining the age of twenty.

16. Q.—A. by statutory deed grants land " to B. for the term of 50 years, and from and after the death of B. to C., his heirs and assigns forever." Is the remainder to C. good ? Why ?

A.—This is a vested remainder and is therefore good. A vested remainder does not require a freehold estate to support it, but a contingent remainder does.

17. Q.—A. owns Whiteacre, but is not in actual possession thereof. A trespasser enters and remains without

acknowledgment for seven years. Then A. mortgages the land to B. and pays interest on his mortgage for six years. During all this time the trespasser remains in possession undisturbed and without acknowledgment. A. having made default the mortgage is foreclosed and the mortgagee demands possession. The trespasser claims title by possession. Who is entitled to the land, and why ?

A.—By statute this is an exception and the possession does not run against the mortgagee, provided the first instalment of interest shall have accrued due and been paid before the trespasser has acquired the legal estate by possession.

R. S. O. c. 111, s. 22.

18. Q.—What is the effect of a mortgagee giving notice of sale under the power in his mortgage upon his other rights under the mortgage ?

A.—When demand of payment is made or notice of intention to exercise power of sale is given, no further proceedings can be taken until expiration of time named in the notice or demand, without order of a Judge.

R. S. O. c. 102, s. 30.

19. Q.—How can you draw a conveyance of land so that the purchaser can convey it free from his wife's dower without requiring her signature ?

A.—You can convey to A. and his heirs to such uses as he shall appoint and until and in default of appointment to A. in fee.

20. Q.—Is a registered memorial of a deed sufficient evidence thereof ? Why ?

tgages the
six years.
possession
A. having
mortgagee
itle by pos-
?

possession
d the first
d been paid
ate by pos-

ving notice
1 his other

r notice of
further pro-
e named in
1.

and so that
rife's dower

uch uses as
ointment to

1fficient evi-

A.—Before the Vendor and Purchaser Act, registered memorials were not sufficient, but now if the deeds are in the possession of the vendor they must be produced or attested copies furnished, but if not in his possession or power the registered memorials of all discharged mortgages and registered memorials twenty years old of other instruments are made primary evidence of the deeds to which they relate where they are executed by the grantor, and in other cases where the possession has been consistent with the registered title.

Armour, p. 88.

R. S. O. c. 112, s. 1, s-s. 1, 2, 3 and 4.

21. Q.—A testator bequeaths $100 to each of the three children of A. As a matter of fact A. has six children. What is the operation of the bequest, if any?

A.—The six children take $100 each.

Hawkins, pp. 63-65.

22. Q.—A devise to A. for life, and after his death to his issue. A. dies in the lifetime of the testator. What becomes of the land which is the subject of the devise?

A.—The land goes to the heirs of A. In a devise of real estate the word "issue" means the "heirs of the body," and therefore A. would take an estate tail if he were living at the time of the testator's death.

Hawkins, p. 189.

23. Q.—What was the meaning of the words "die without issue," in a will before the Will's Act, and what is the meaning now?

A.—The words "die without issue" in a will before the Wills Act meant a failure of issue at the time of death or any time afterwards ; but now it means a failure of issue at death and not an indefinite failure of issue ; unless an intention appear to the contrary in either case.

Hawkins, pp. 205 and 214.

R. S. O. c. 109, s. 32.

24. Q.—A. sells and conveys land to B. who keeps the deed without registering it. An execution against the lands of A. is placed in the Sheriff's hands and then B. registers his conveyance. Is the land affected by the writ ? Why ?

A.—No. As soon as a conveyance is delivered the estate passes to the grantee, and a writ against the lands of the vendor, placed in the Sheriff's hands after delivery but before registration of the deed, will not bind them.

Russell v. *Russell, 28 Gr. 419.*

Bank of Montreal v. *Baker, 9 Gr. at p. 107.*

Armour, p. 128.

Park v. *Riley, 12 Gr. 69*, decides that a vendor's interest after he has made a contract for sale is not exigible under a writ against lands.

25. Q.—A mortgagee assigns his mortgage by endorsement on the mortgage. The assignee does not register. Subsequently the mortgagor pays the mortgagee, who gives a discharge but tells the mortgagor that he has mislaid the mortgage. The discharge is registered. The assignee then applies to the mortgagor for payment and ascertains what has been done. What relief is the assignee entitled to as against the mortgagor or the mortgagee ?

A.—He has no right against the mortgagor for he should have notified him, but he can recover against the mortgagee for money had and received.

26. Q.—Is a mortgagor entitled to take proceedings to quiet the title to the mortgaged premises under the Quieting Titles Act ?

A.—Owners in fee simple, or trustees for the sale of the fee simple may obtain judicial investigation of title. In case of any other estate the investigation is discretionary with a Judge.

R. S. O. c. 113, ss. 2 and 3.

27. Q.—Can a mortgagee charge on the land premiums paid by him for fire insurance ?

A.—Yes, if there is a covenant to insure in the mortgage, but otherwise he cannot as to deeds executed before March, 1879, but such a clause is now deemed part of the mortgage unless otherwise excluded.

R. S. O., c. 102, s. 18, s-s. 2.

28. Q.—A tenant whose term expired on the 1st of August remains in possession and claims the right to harvest the crops which would mature during August and September. Has he this right ?   Why ?

A.—No ; the tenant knew his term was to expire on the first day of August, and he should have governed himself accordingly.

29. Q.—Under a gift by will to the next of kin of testator, who will take ?

A.—The nearest blood relations in equal degree will take, as, father, mother, and children, who take together as joint tenants.   This is not equivalent to next of kin according to the " Statutes of Distributions."

Hawkins, pp. 91 and 97.

80. Q.—A devise of "the use and *occupation*" of the testator's house. What interest will the devisee take, and subject to what, if any, conditions?

A.—The devisee will take an estate for life, not subject to the condition of residence. The word " occupation " is extremely material, as in the legal sense it denotes possession or ownership, not the act of inhabiting.

Hawkins, p. 119.

81. Q.—What characteristic difference is there between the covenants for title contained in the Statutory short form of deed and those contained in the Statutory short form of mortgage?

A.—The covenants in a Statutory short form of deed extend only to the last purchaser, but in a Statutory short form of mortgage they are absolute, and extend back of the mortgagor and last purchaser.

82. Q.—A purchaser of land from B. has paid his purchase money and taken a conveyance without notice of any encumbrance. Before registering it he is notified by A. that he, A., is entitled to a vendor's lien for purchase money due him by B. .fe finds on registry a deed from A. to B., which contains an acknowledgment by A. that he has received the full consideration from B. There is no registered instrument securing A.'s purchase money. The purchaser registered his conveyance. Is A. entitled to enforce his lien as against the purchaser?

A.—No.

R. S. O., c. 114, s. 83.

83. Q.—After a deed of land has been delivered to a purchaser, who has paid his purchase money, the parties

agree to rescind the whole contract. The vendor returns the purchase money, and the purchaser returns the deed, which is immediately destroyed. What is the effect? Explain fully.

A.—The property had vested in the purchaser, and he should reconvey to the vendor. By the destruction of the deed the vendor's covenants were destroyed, but as the property had vested this would not amount to a recision of the contract and a re-transfer of the property.

34. Q.—A policy of insurance against fire is assigned with a mortgage of the premises to the mortgagee, nothing being said as to the application of the insurance money in case of a loss. Before the mortgage matures a loss happens. How may the insurance money be applied? State the respective rights of the mortgagee and mortgagor.

A.—See R. S. O. c. 102, s. 4.

35. Q.—A devise "to the relations of A." Who will take?

A.—A devise or bequest to the "relations" of A. or of the testator is construed to mean the persons who would be entitled under the *Statutes of Distributions* either as next of kin or by representation to next of kin.

Hawkins, p. 102.

36. Q.—A devises to one who is a bastard, without words of limitation or inheritance. Does the devisee take a fee simple or a fee tail? Why?

A.—The devisee takes a fee simple, but if words of inheritance had been used the devisee would have taken a fee tail, since the only heirs he could have would be the heirs of the body. However, this is doubted by some, and the general opinion now seems to be that, by R. S. O., c. 109, s. 4, the bastard would take whatever interest the grantor had.

37. Q.—Which is the most advantageous way of pleading a prescriptive right? and why?

A.—There are three ways of pleading a prescriptive right, viz.: (a) By lost grant, (b) by immemorial user, (c) by length of possession. The first is the most advantageous, because it is more easily proven than the others.

Broom, p. 862.

38. Q.—A will is made by an infant, who dies after attaining his majority. Is the will valid? Why?

A.—No. It is contrary to the Statute.

R. S. O. c. 109, s. 11.

39. Q.—What purpose does the *habendum* serve in a conveyance? Is it essential?

A.—The *habendum* is a non-essential formality expressing the extent of the grantor's interest in the thing granted. It may abridge, qualify or enlarge the premises, but where they are repugnant the premises will operate in preference to the *habendum*.

Wharton's Law Lexicon, p. 220, f.

40. Q.—A conveyance to X. to the use of A. for and during his natural life, and from and after his death to the use of X. in trust to the heirs of A. .What estate does A. take?

A.—A. takes a life estate, and X. takes a fee simple in trust for the heirs of A., subject to A.'s life estate.

41. Q.—What is the present state of the law as to the validity or invalidity of voluntary conveyances as against subsequent purchasers for value ?

A.—Before *31 Vic. c. 9* a voluntary deed was void against a subsequent purchaser for value, but now a *bona fide* voluntary deed, if registered before execution of a subsequent conveyance for value is good.

Armour, p. 74.

42. Q.—What are the four cardinal rules for the construction of wills ?

A.—(1) Ascertain the *expressed intentions* of the testator, *i.e.*, the intention which the will itself, either expressly or by implication, declares ; or the meaning which the words of the will, properly interpreted, convey.

(2) The words and expressions used are to be taken in their *ordinary, proper* and *grammatical* sense.

(3) *Technical* words and expressions must be taken in their *technical* sense unless there is a clear intention to the contrary.

(4) Notwithstanding 2 and 3, the intention of the testator, as collected from the will with the aid of admissible extrinsic evidence, must have effect given to it beyond and even against the literal sense of particular words and expressions. The intention, when legitimately proved, is competent not only to *fix* the sense of *ambiguous* words, but to *control* the sense even of *clear* words, and to supply the place of *express* words, in cases of difficulty or ambiguity. (Aid to memory : *Iota*, (I) Intention, (O) Ordinary sense, (T) Technical words, (A) Ambiguous words.)

Hawkins, pp. 1, 2, 3 and 4.

43. Q.—Is it necessary for the witnesses to a will to sign in the presence of each other ?

A.—Yes, before 1874.

R. S. O. c. 109, s. 5.

Since 1874 it is necessary for the witnesses to sign in the presence of the testator, but not in the presence of each other.

R. S. O. c. 109, s. 12, s-s. 1.

44. Q.—What is the *prima facie* meaning of the word "family" in a bequest ?   What in a devise ?

A.—A bequest of personal estate to the "family" of A. *prima facie* means his children (not A. himself or his wife). In a devise of real estate the word "family" will generally be construed as "heirs" or "heirs of the body." A devise to "A. and his family" gives A. an estate tail.

Hawkins, p. 89.

45. Q.—What is the rule as to repeated legacies.   (1) When they occur in separate testamentary instruments as a will and codicil ?   (2) When they occur in one instrument ?

A.—(1) When they occur in separate testamentary instruments the general rule is that the legatee takes both.

(2) When they occur in one instrument the general rule is that the legatee takes only one.

Hawkins, p. 303.

(1) Under different instruments legacies, whether equal or unequal, are cumulative, unless the same motive and the same sum be expressed.

(2) Under the same instrument—(a) Equal legacies are substitutive.   *Greenwood* v. *Greenwood, 1 Bro. C. C. 31 n.* (b) Unequal legacies are cumulative.

Snell p. 277.

46. Q.—A mortgagor dies after the 1st of July, 1886, intestate, leaving a widow and infant children. No letters of administration are taken out. How do we proceed to foreclose or sell ?

A.—The Devolution of Estates Act vests the legal estate in the personal representatives. The Short Forms Act uses the word heirs. Hence, to avoid doubts in consequence of the former Act power should be reserved to the personal representatives of the mortgagee, and provision should be made for giving notice to the personal representative of the mortgagor, and if none appointed the power should be exercisable without notice.

Armour, p. 265.

To obtain foreclosure or sale by action it would be necessary to apply to the Court for the appointment of an administrator *ad litem* to represent the estate of the mortgagor.

47. Q.—What are the provisions of the Conveyancing and Law of Property Act of 1886 with respect to Limitations of Estates ?

A.—Words of limitation are now unnecessay, the grantee taking all the interest of the grantor. By statute the words *fee simple, in tail, in tail male* or *in tail female*, are quite sufficient.

R. S. O., c. 109, s. 4, and c. 100, s. 4.

48. Q.—Having obtained judgment against a debtor, you find that he owns a piece of land, part of which is in the County of York and part in the adjoining County of Ontario, the whole piece being mortgaged. How can you realize the judgment debt out of this land ?

A.—You cannot recover under execution, for neither Sheriff could seize more than a portion, and, as the property is mortgaged, the equity of redemption is not divisible. You might apply to the Court for a *Receiver*, or for equitable execution ; or you might commence an action for the sale of the property.

Armour, p. 180.

49. Q.—At a sale of mortgaged lands under a power of sale in the mortgage what persons are debarred from buying.

A.—The mortgagee or his agent (which includes his Solicitor or his Solicitor's clerk) cannot purchase at the sale.

In *Martinson* v. *Clowes, L. R. 21 Ch. D. at p. 857,* the Secretary of a Building Society, who were mortgagees, bought at auction on his own account, and the sale was set aside at the instance of the mortgagor, though the price given was a fair one.

Armour, p. 282.

50. Q.—A grant of land in fee simple to A. B., C. B. his wife and D. E.   How do they take?

A.—A. B. and C. B. his wife will take one moiety and D. E. the other.

Hawkins, p. 115.

However, since the Married Woman's Property Act of 1884, the tendency of the decisions in such grants is to give the wife a share separate from her husband.

51. Q.—A devise to "A. and his children," A. having no children at the time of the devise.   What interest does A. take?

A.—A devise of real estate to A. *and his children*, A. having no children at the time of the devise, vests in A. an estate tail; " Children " being construed as a word of limitation.

Wild's Case.

Hawkins, p. 198.

52. Q.—A devise or bequest to " the children of A. and B. as tenants in common." How do they take ?

A.—B. and the children of A. take as tenants in common *per capita*.

Under a devise or bequest to " the children of A. and *of* B." as tenants in common, *prima facie* the children take *per capita*, not *per stirpes*. If the gift be to " the children of A. and B." it has been held that it is a gift to B. and not to his children on account of the non-repetition of the word " of " before the word B. But although it may be more idiomatic to speak of " the children of A. and of B.," it may perhaps be doubted whether usage requires the repetition of the particle, and in later cases this view has been followed.

Hawkins, p. 113.

53. Q.—State the nature of a Mechanic's Lien. How does it arise, and how is it preserved against land ?

A.—See R. S. O., c. 126.

54. Q.—What is the rule as to computation of interest on an overdue mortgage, when no provision as to the rate after maturity is made by the instrument ? Does the form of action make any difference in the mode or rate of computation ?

Q.A.—2

A.—The rule is that six *per cent.* is chargeable after maturity. If you proceed by *power of sale* or *foreclosure* you can only recover this rate after maturity, but, if you sue on the covenant and claim damages at the former rate of interest, it will be in the discretion of the Court to allow it.

55. Q.—What is the object of registering a deed or mortgage? Explain fully.

A.—Registration is notice to all parties dealing with the property subsequently. Unregistered instruments, after grant from the Crown, are void against a subsequent registered purchaser.

R. S. O., c. 114, s. 76.

56. Q.—A vendor dies intestate. The purchaser desires to have the contract specifically performed. How would you proceed, and what parties would you make?

A.—The purchaser can sue the personal representatives of the vendor. If none are appointed he can apply to the Court for an administrator *ad litem*.

R. S. O., c. 110, s. 15.

57. Q.—What was and what is now the value as to a mortgagor's right to inspect the title deeds?

A.—Since the 1st of July, 1886, the mortgagor, as long as his right to redeem subsists, can, at reasonable times, on request, and at his own cost, see and make copies of the title deeds.

R. S. O., c. 102, s. 3.

58. Q.—When a trustee dies and no provision is made by the trust deed for appointing a new trustee, can one be appointed without applying to the Court?

A.—Yes.

> R. S. O., c. 110, s. 3.

59. Q.—What investments of trust funds may trustees lawfully make in Ontario when there is no direction in the trust instrument concerning investments?

A.—Trust funds may be invested in Dominion and Provincial securities. and also in certain companies incorporated with a capital of a $100,000.00 as authorized by Statute, or in securities which are a first charge on land held in fee simple.

> R. S. O., c. 110, ss. 29 and 30.

60. Q.—What are the provisions of the Registry Act as to notice?

A.—Registration of any instrument shall constitute notice of the instrument to all persons claiming any interest in the lands subsequent to such registration.

> R. S. O., c. 114, s. 80.

61. Q.—A purchase of land is completed by payment of the purchase money and delivery of conveyance. Before registering the latter the purchaser gets actual notice that there is an undischarged mortgage on the land which has never been registered. He immediately registers his conveyance and subsequently the mortgage is registered. Is the purchaser affected by the mortgage? If so what remedy has he?

A.—Yes, because he had actual notice of it before registration. The mortgage would have priority but the purchaser would have his remedy against the vendor. (Compare Question No. 32).

By the Registry Act, "priority of registration shall prevail, unless before such prior registration there has been actual notice of the prior instrument by the party claiming under the prior registration."

Armour, p. 75.

62. Q.—A. holds lands in trust to pay the rents and profits to X. for life, and after his death to divide amongst the children of X. Upon X.'s death the children desire to sell, and direct the trustee to convey, they all joining in the conveyance. It appears that there is an execution in the sheriff's hands against the goods and lands of one of the children. Will it affect the purchasers? Why?

A.—No ; execution will not attach when there is a beneficial interest in land held by several persons, and the execution is only against one of them.

R. S. O., c. 64, s. 25.

Armour, p. 132.

63. Q.—What are the provisions of the Vendor and Purchaser Act as to evidence of deeds and mortgages which cannot be produced by the vendor ?

A.—This will not be a valid objection to the title in case the purchaser will, on completion of the contract, have an equitable right to the production of such documents.

R. S. O., c. 112, s. 1, (4).

In actions it shall not be necessary to produce any evidence which, by section 1 of the Vendor and Purchaser Act, is dispensed with as between vendor and purchaser, and the evidence therein declared to be sufficient as between vendor and purchaser shall be *prima facie* sufficient for the purposes of such actions.

R. S. O., c. 112, s. 2.

64. Q.—Upon death intestate after the 1st of July, 1886, of the owner of land, how can the land be sold? Who should make the conveyance?

A.—Now all property devolves upon and becomes vested in the legal personal representatives, and they are the proper persons to make the sale of and convey the land.

R. S. O., c. 108, s. 4 (1) and s. 9.

65. Q.—A devise of the use and occupation of "my Lakeside Farm." The testator had within two or three years of his death purchased several small parcels of land adjoining the farm, and had cultivated them as he had been in the habit of cultivating the farm. Would they pass under the devise? Why?

A.—It is a doubtful question. In *Webb* v. *Byng* the decision was that the small parcels would not pass under the devise, but Hawkins thinks that if the question were decided again it might be otherwise.

Hawkins, p. 21.

66. Q.—When a sale is made of an equity of redemption under an execution can the mortgagee bid? What is the effect of his becoming a purchaser at such a sale?

A.—The mortgagee can bid, and if he becomes the purchaser he shall give to the mortgagor a release of the mortgage debt.

R. S. O., c. 64, s. 64.

67. Q.—A conveyance is made to A. for life, and from and after his death to X., his heirs and assigns to the use of the heirs of A., their heirs and assigns forever. What disposition can A. make of the land in his lifetime? What

becomes of it on his death, if no disposition of it is made by him?

A.—A. has a *fee simple*, and can dispose of it during his lifetime. If no disposition of it be made during his lifetime, then it goes to his heirs direct after his death.

68. Q.—How is a registered purchaser affected by outstanding equitable interests in the land?

A.—Equitable liens and charges shall not prevail in any Court against a registered instrument.

(Compare Question No. 32.)

 R. S. O., c. 114, s. 83.

69. Q.—When a mortgagor leases the mortgaged lands, what relation does the tenant bear to the mortgagee, and what are their relative rights and liabilities?

A.—As to his liability to the mortgagee in respect of rent, and as to his relations to the mortgagee, see

 Leith, p. 218.

70. Q.—A conveyance of land in Ottawa is drawn in the French language, and on presentation to the Registrar he refuses to register it. Is he bound to do so? Why?

A.—Yes. There is no provision as to what language the deed must be drawn in, and in the absence of this the Registrar is bound to accept it.

71. Q.—A. buys a piece of land from B. which is mortgaged for $500. The price of the land agreed on is $1,500. The consideration inserted in the deed is $1,000. The short form is used, the only variation being that the covenants for title except from their operation the mortgage. There is nothing said about assuming liability for the mortgage. Is A. bound to pay it all? Why?

A.—A. buys subject to the mortgage for $500, which can be recovered out of the property. A., however, does not make any covenant to pay the $500, but B. remains liable on his covenant in the mortgage.

72. Q.—A piece of land is sold under an execution against the owner. His wife, after his death, claims dower. Is she entitled to it? Why?

A.—Yes. Being the sale of the debtor's interest alone it will not affect his wife's dower.

Walker v. *Powers, R. and J. Digest*, p. 1125.
Armour, p. 263.

73. Q.—To what covenant is a purchaser entitled on a purchase from a trustee?

A.—He is entitled only to the covenant that the trustee has done no act to incumber.

74. Q.—A testator on his deathbed reads over his will, which has been drawn according to his instructions, and approves of it. He begins to write his name, but through weakness desists and dies without having again attempted to sign. Is the will valid, there being no objection on other grounds?

A.—No.

R. S. O., c. 109, s. 12.

75.—What is the effect of a devise to a married woman for her separate use, her husband being a witness to the will?

A.—It is null and void.

R. S. O., c. 109, s. 17.

76. Q.—The Devolution of Estates Act, 1886, declares that land shall rest in the personal representative of a person dying after the 1st of July, 1886. Should you therefore limit an estate to a man and his executors, etc., or to a man and his heirs?

A.—By Statute the personal representatives are to be deemed in law heirs and assigns.

R. S. O., c. 108, s. 10.

77. Q.—After a mortgagor is in default, how long has the mortgagee in which to bring (1) an action to recover the land, (2) an action on the covenant?

A.—(1) The mortgagee may enter or bring an action to recover such land at any time within ten years from the last payment, although more than ten years may have elapsed since default.

R. S. O., c. 111, s. 12.

(2) The mortgagee may bring an action on the covenant at any time within ten years.

R. S. O., c. 111, s. 23.

Kingsford's Manual of Evidence, p. 106.

78. Q.—Can executors lawfully carry on the testator's business? If so, to what extent are they justified in using the moneys of the estate.

A.—The executors can lawfully carry on the testator's business if so directed by the will, but must not use the moneys of the estate beyond the amount set aside for that purpose in the will. It must be noted, however, that the executors are personally liable in all cases.

79. Q.—Can a married woman make a will? If so, by what authority?

A.—By the *Married Women's Property Act*, a married woman shall be capable of acquiring, holding and disposing by will or otherwise, of any real or personal property as her separate property, in the same manner as if she were a *feme sole*, without the intervention of any trustee.

R. S. O., c. 182, s. 3 (1).

80. Q.—Will the word " effects " used in a will include real property ?

A.—The word " effects " is confined to personal estate and does not include real estate unless an intention appear to the contrary.

Hawkins, p. 54.

In Ontario the word " effects " carries realty unless otherwise controlled.

Hamill v. *Hamill*, 6 *Ont. R. p. 681.*

81. Q.—A bequest of an annuity is made without any indication in the will of the length of time it is to continue. What interest will the annuitant take ?   Explain.

A. —A bequest of an annuity, not existing before, to A., simpliciter, is *prima facie* for life only.

Hawkins, p. 124.

82. Q.—A., owning two houses, with their back walls (in which there are no doors) to the street, sells one to B. There is a carriage drive from the street alongside the house retained by A. and over land belonging to him, to the front of the house sold to B., but no other way of getting to and from the street, as B.'s house adjoins on the other sides the lands of other people.   There is no express grant of a way in the conveyance.   Has B. any and what right of way over A.'s land ?

A.—B. must have some way to get out from his house, and the law says that he has a right of way over the land of the vendor by necessity.

Armour, p. 161.

83. Q.—An agreement is made to buy land, purchase money to be payable in ten equal annual instalments, upon payment of the last of which the conveyance is to be made. Nothing is said in the agreement as to title. What are the purchaser's rights as to title ?

A.—The purchaser has a right to demand a good title to be shown either before he pays any of the instalments, or after he has paid part of them, i.e., the vendor must show that he will be able to give a good title when the proper time comes for making the conveyance.

84. Q.—Bearing in mind the provisions of the Devolution of Estates Act, how should a power of sale in a mortgage be now drawn so as to give the mortgagee full power to exercise it in case of the mortgagor's death ?

A.—Provision should be made for giving notice to the personal representatives of the mortgagor, and, if no personal representatives be appointed, then that the power should be exercised without notice.

Armour, p. 265.

85. Q.—Where there are successive independent trespassers on land for a sufficient length of time in the aggregate to bar the true owner, but no one trespasser has been in possession for ten years, in whom is the title to the land ?

A.—The title to the land is in the last trespasser.

Dixon v. *Gayfere, 17 Beav. 430.*

But *Asher* v. *Whitlock*, a common law case, decides that the trespasser who had prior possession may eject the last one. Now, however, in cases of conflict equity prevails.

Armour, p. 203.

But *Short* v. *Security Co.*, decided in 1889 in the Privy Council, is a later case, and it was there held that none of the trespassers were entitled, but that the title still remains in the true owner.

86. Q.—A. B. having no title to a piece of land makes a conveyance thereof, and the grantee registers it. What remedy, if any, has the true owner?

A.—This is a bastard deed. Where a deed appears upon the register made by a person who has no apparent title, the Courts have held that the owner of the land has a right to its cancellation.

Armour, p. 133.

87. Q.—What is the difference between " showing " and " making " a good title?

A.—A title is " shown " when the abstract states all the matters which, if proved, make a good title.

A title is " made " when those matters are proved.

Armour, p. 40.

88. Q.—Define " marketable title," " safe-holding title," and " doubtful title."

A.—A " marketable title " is one you can force on an unwilling purchaser at all times and under all circumstances.

A " safe-holding title " is perfectly good, but you may not be able to adduce the proper proofs of its sufficiency, and you could not force it on an unwilling purchaser.

A " doubtful title " is one that is not marketable, and one concerning which the Court is not able to form a clear opinion. A purchaser is not bound to accept it.

Armour. pp. 2 and 8.

89. Q.—A devisee since the Devolution of Estates Act registers the will by delivering a sworn copy to the Registrar. He then offers the land for sale. Can he make a good title on his own conveyance ? Why ?

A.—No. The personal representatives must join since all property devolves upon them.

R. S. O., c. 108, s. 4, s-s. 1, and s. 8.

90. Q.—A will is witnessed by three witnesses (two being sufficient) one of whom is a legatee. What is the effect upon the attestation and upon his legacy ?

A.—The legatee who was a witness cannot take under the will but the attestation is not affected.

R. S. O., c. 109, s. 17.

91. Q.—What is the effect of altering the text of a will after execution ?

A.—See R. S. O., c. 109, s. 28.

92. Q.—How should a necessary alteration of a will be made in order to place its validity beyond dispute ?

A.—See R. S. O., c. 109, s. 28.

93. Q.—When can you have a certificate of *lis pendens* set aside on motion without a trial of the action ?

A.—When the plaintiff abandons his action, or when the amount claimed is paid into court, the certificate will be vacated. Also see last Ont. Stat., 1890.

94. Q.—When an open contract for the sale of land is made and it is discovered that there is an encumbrance on the land, what are the purchaser's rights respecting the same ? If the encumbrancer is not bound to release and will not do so, what course can be pursued to complete the contract ?

A.—The purchaser can have the encumbrance removed ; and if the encumbrancer is not bound to release he can pay the purchase money into court and thus make a fund sufficient to satisfy the encumbrance.

Armour, pp. 114 and 115.

95. Q.—What is meant by saying that an abstract should commence with a good root of title ? Give examples of instruments which do not form a good root.

A.—The abstract should go back sixty years, unless there is a patent from the Crown or an order under the Quieting Titles Act within that time, and in selecting a document for the commencement of the abstract, care should be taken not to select one which refers to any anterior assurance or depends upon it for its validity. For instance neither a settlement made in pursuance of articles nor a deed exercising a power is a good root ; for it is not certain that the settlement is prepared conformably to the articles or that the power was properly exercised.

Armour, p. 29.

96. Q.—What leases are required to be registered so as to preserve priority ?

A.—Every lease for a longer term than seven years must be registered. A lease for four years with a covenant for

a renewal for a term, which in all would exceed seven
years, need not be registered if the lessee is in possession ;
and the lessee would be entitled against a mortgagee who
registered during the first term of the lease.   The possession which is required of the lessee is possession under the
lease by which he claims his renewal of term ; a present
possession and a lease for a term to commence *in futuro*
would not prevail against a conveyance registered before
the commencement of the term.

Armour, pp. 57 *et seq.*

97. Q.—What is a bare trustee ?

A.—A bare trustee is a mere depositary of the legal
estate.   If he has any beneficial interest in the land he is
not a bare trustee.

Armour, p. 220.

98. Q.—What leases must be made by deed in order to
be valid ?

A.—A lease for more than three years must be by deed,
but an agreement for a lease for three years need not be by
deed but must be in writing.   A lease not exceeding three
years at two thirds of rack rent is not required to be in
writing by the Statute of Frauds.   All leases required to
be in writing by the Statute of Frauds must be by ed by
our statute.

(N. B.—Twenty-seven repeated questions have been
excluded from this collection on Real Property and Wills.
Some have been repeated once, others twice, and a few have
been repeated three and four times.—F. L. W.)

CHAPTER II.

CONTRACTS AND SALES.

1. Q.—Is an infant liable—(a) on an account stated when the account consists of the price of necessities; (b) for money lent to him for the purpose of enabling him to purchase necessaries, and which he has used for that purpose; (c) on a promissory note given by him for the price of necessaries?

A.—(a) No, an infant is not liable on an account stated when the account consists of the price of necessaries. The supply of necessaries to an infant creates only a liability on a simple contract and it cannot be made the ground of any different kind of liability. This is an exception to the general rule that an infant is incapable to bind himself by contract. It is not for the benefit of the trader who may trust an infant, but for the benefit of the infant himself.

(b) At common law a loan of money could not be deemed equivalent to necessaries though actually spent on necessaries.

(c) Such is also the common law with regard to negotiable instruments. But it is said that a bill or note given by an infant to a creditor for necessaries may be valid if it is not payable to order or negotiable.

Pollock, pp. 138 and 143.

2. Q.—A written agreement is made between two persons by which one is to serve the other for six months from

date, performing the duties and receiving the wages therein specified. On the following day they agree verbally that some of the duties specified in the writing are to be omitted, and others not specified are to be performed instead thereof. On the trial of an action for breach of the written agreement, will parol evidence be admitted to prove that it was varied by the subsequent verbal agreement? Give reasons.

A.—Yes. Parol evidence, that the written contract was varied by the subsequent verbal agreement, will be a good defence to the action for breach of the written agreement, if he can show that the written contract does not express the real agreement: and this whether the contract is of a kind required by law to be in writing or not. This contract is only for a term of six months, and need not be in writing under the Statute of Frauds.

(Compare Question No. 20 *post.*)

  Pollock, p. 508.

3. Q.—A resident of Ontario purchases goods in Buffalo from a merchant of that city, and then smuggles them into Ontario, the vendor being aware at the time of sale of the purchaser's intention to smuggle. (1) Can the vendor recover the price of the goods in an Ontario Court? (2) Will it make any difference if the vendor pack the goods in a particular way so as to assist the purchaser in smuggling them? Give reasons.

A.—(1) Yes. (2) The vendor cannot recover if he aids the smuggling.

The sale was complete abroad, and will therefore be governed by foreign law. It was not immoral or illegal in Buffalo, because no country takes notice of the revenue laws of another country. The goods were not sold to be

;es therein
rbally that
e omitted,
nd thereof.
:ten agree-
that it was
;e reasons.

utract was
be a good
agreement,
not express
ract is of a
is contract
in writing

in Buffalo
them into
sale of the
he vendor
ourt? (2)
ic goods in
smuggling

if he aids

erefore be
l or illegal
he revenue
sold to be

delivered in Ontario, but they were actually delivered in Buffalo. But, however, if he aids the smuggling, he then becomes amenable to our revenue laws ; and as smuggling is illegal here, he cannot therefore recover the price of the goods in an Ontario Court.

Waymel v. *Reed, T. R. p. 599.*

Benjamin, p. 503.

4. Q.—Is the receipt of goods by a carrier an acceptance and actual receipt, or either of them, by the purchaser, within the meaning of the 17th section of the Statute of Frauds? Why?

A.—The carrier is agent of the buyer to receive delivery but not to accept, under the Statute of Frauds. Delivery to the carrier constitutes *actual receipt* by the purchaser but not *acceptance.*

Benjamin, pp. 143-155.

5. Q.—Can a vendor who keeps possession of goods by virtue of his lien for unpaid purchase money recover from the purchaser storage, or other charges, for the time he so keeps them? Why?

A.—The vendor's lien extends only to the price of goods, and does not extend to storage or other charges. The vendor's remedy for these charges, if any, is personal against the buyer. It would not be right to charge for keeping the goods when he did it for his own benefit. In *Somes* v. *The British Empire Shipping Company*, it was held that a shipwright who kept a ship in his dock after repairing her, in order to preserve his lien, had no claim at all for dock charges against the owner of the ship for the time that elapsed between the completion of the repairs and the delivery of the ship, notwithstanding the owner's default in payment.

> Benjamin, p. 782.

Q.—Will a mere proposal to sell goods on the terms therein specified constitute a sufficient memorandum of a bargain within the Statute of Frauds? If so, when?

A.—Yes; a mere proposal to sell goods on the terms therein specified will be a sufficient memorandum of a bargain within the Statute of Frauds, if it is supplemented by parol proof of acceptance.

> Benjamin, p. 218.

7. Q.—State briefly when a vendor will, and when he will not, be deprived of the right of *stoppage in transitu* by having taken a bill or note for the price of goods.

A.—He will be deprived of his right to *stoppage in transitu* if he accepts them as an absolute payment; but the vendor's right will not be lost in consequence of his having received conditional payment by bills of exchange or other securities, even though he may have negotiated the bills so that they are outstanding in third hands unmatured.

> Benjamin, p. 822.

8. Q.—After goods have been delivered to the vendee on a credit sale, the vendor, not receiving the price at the time agreed on, tortiously retakes the goods. What are the respective rights and remedies of the parties under these circumstances?

A.—The vendee can maintain an action of trover for the conversion, and the vendor can counter-claim for the price of the goods. If, however, from the nature of the contract or dealings between the parties, the vendor is unable to maintain an action or set up a counter-claim for the price, then the vendee's damages in trover will only be the actual damages, *i.e.*, the value of the goods less the price due.

Benjamin, p. 774.

9. Q.—What difference does it make as to the right of the vendor to recover the price of goods sold from the vendee whether the property in the goods has passed to the vendee or not ?

A.—If the property in the goods has passed to the vendee, then the vendor loses his lien and can only maintain an action for the price. If the property in the goods has passed to the vendee, but not the actual possession, and the vendor has not waived his lien, he may still exercise his lien and recover his price, if the vendee becomes insolvent or does not pay at the time agreed. If the property in the goods has not passed, the vendor may have an action for breach of the contract, or he may exercise his lien upon them for the price and refuse to deliver until he gets his pay.

10. Q.—Give examples of *executed* and *executory* considerations respectively, and state what is the essential requisite of the former as distinguished from the latter in simple contracts ?

A.—*Executed consideration :* A. bails a man's servant and afterwards the master promises to indemnify A. *Executory consideration:* The master promises to indemnify A. in the event of his bailing his servant. *Executed considera-*

tion will not suffice to support a contract unless at the
request of the promissor.

Wharton's Law Lexicon, p. 168.

11. Q.—What is the law as to the validity of a contract
of sale of goods when the purchaser is under the influence
of liquor at the time the contract is made ?

A.—A *drunkard*, when in a state of complete intoxication, so as not to know what he is doing, has no capacity to
contract in general, but he would be liable for absolute
necessaries supplied to him while in that condition ; and
Pollock, C.B., put the ground of the liability as follows :
" A contract may be implied by law in many cases, even
where the party protested against any contract.   The law
says he did contract because he ought to have done so.   On
that ground the creditor might recover against him when
sober, for necessaries supplied to him when drunk."

But a contract entered into by a person who is so drunk
as not to know what he is doing, is voidable only and not
void, and may therefore be ratified by him when he becomes
sober.

Benjamin, pp. 32 and 33.

12. Q.—What is the difference in legal effect between a
warranty given by a vendor at the time of sale of goods and
one given after the sale, and what is the reason of the
difference ?

A.—A warranty at the time of the sale is good, but a
warranty after the sale is completed is not good, because
there is nothing to support the subsequent agreement to
warrant.

Benjamin, p. 606.

s at the

a contract
influence

intoxica-
capacity to
r absolute
ition ; and
is follows :
cases, even
. The law
oue so. On
him when
ak."

is so drunk
ily and not
he becomes

between a
f goods and
ason of the

good, but a
od, because
greement to

13. Q.—In the case of a contract of sale of goods within the Statute of Frauds, how will the validity of the contract be affected (a) by the fact that no price is either mentioned in the writing or agreed on verbally, (b) by the fact that a price is agreed on verbally but not mentioned in the writing ?

A.—(a) When nothing is said as to price the law implies a reasonable price, and the contract in this case would be valid.

(b) In *Elmore* v. *Kingscote*, the Court held that the verbal agreement on the price was a material part of the bargain, and, as it was not mentioned in the writing, the memorandum was insufficient under the Statute and the contract was invalid.

Benjamin, pp. 214 and 215.

14. Q.—A retailer buys from a wholesale merchant ten bales of hops *as per sample*. The hops are unmerchantable from some latent defect unknown to the vendor, and not discoverable upon a simple examination. Has the purchaser any remedy, and if so, what ?

A.—The purchaser has a right to reject the hops and recover the loss of profit which would have accrued if the hops had been without any latent defect. Compare the case of *Heilbutt* v. *Hickson*, *L. R. 7 C. P. 438.*

Benjamin, pp. 639 *et seq.*

15. Q.—What effect has the taking by a vendor of the purchaser's note for the price of goods sold upon a vendor's right to sue the purchaser for such price ?

A.—If the vendor takes a note payable at a future day

he cannot legally commence an action on his original debt until such note becomes payable and default is made in the payment.

16. Q.—On April 1st A. sold and delivered a horse to B., receiving his cheque for the price on a bank where B. falsely and fraudulently represented he had funds, having in fact none. On April 2nd B. sold and delivered the horse to C., an innocent purchaser, for value, and received the price. On April 3rd A., having presented the cheque and found that he had been defrauded out of the amount, went at once to C. and demanded the horse, which was refused. Has A. any, and if so what, remedy against C. ? Give reasons fully.

A.—This is a case in which B. obtained the horse by false pretenses, and A. intended to transfer both the property in and the possession of the horse to B., the person guilty of the fraud, and the property passed, however fraudulent the device. The contract would be *voidable* at the election of the vendor, but not void *ab initio*. The vendor may affirm it and sue for the price, or rescind it and sue in trover for the horse. But in the meantime, and until he elects, if B. transfers the horse to an innocent third person for value, the rights of A. will be subordinate to such innocent third person. Therefore in this case A. will have no remedy against C.

Benjamin, pp. 393 *et seq.*

17. Q.—What is the difference in legal effect between a gift of chattels by mere word of mouth and a gift of chattels by deed ?

A.—A parol gift must be accompanied by delivery, but a gift by deed need not be.

Benjamin, p. 3 (7).

18. Q.—A., a Toronto merchant, on November 1st mailed a letter to B., a Kingston merchant, offering him certain goods at certain prices. B. on Nov. 2nd, at 10 a.m., mailed at Kingston a letter to A. accepting this offer. This letter was received by A. in due course on November 3rd. On November 1st, some hours after mailing his offer, A. mailed a letter to B. revoking the offer. This letter went by the next mail after and was received by B. in due course on November 2nd at 4 p.m. Is there any contract binding on A. ?

A.—Yes; the contract was complete at 10 a.m. on November 2nd, and it could not be revoked afterwards by a letter received at 4 p.m.

19. Q.—Will a debt, otherwise barred by the Statute of Limitations, be taken out of the Statute (*a*) by a writing signed by the debtor in which he acknowledges the debt and says that he will never pay it, (*b*) by a writing signed by the debtor promising to pay the debt on a certain condition ? Why ?

A.—The modern law has been concisely stated by Mellish, L.J. "There must be one of three things to take the case out of the Statute. Either there must be an acknowledgment of the debt, from which a promise to pay is to be implied ; or secondly, there must be an unconditional promise to pay the debt; or thirdly, there must be a conditional promise to pay the debt, and evidence that the condition has been performed." A promise to pay as a debt of honor is insufficient, as it excludes the admission of legal liability. When the promise is implied it must be as an inference of fact, not of law.

Pollock, pp. 631-633.

The acknowledgment of a debt with a disclaimer will not take it out the Statute.

Pollock, p. 233, f. n. 8.

20. Q.—A. and B. enter into a written contract by which A. is to work six days each week for a period of three cars from the date of the contract and is to receive (for $24.00 per week. A few days afterwards they verbally agree that A. shall only work five days each week and receive only $20.00 per week. In an action for specific performance of the contract will either party be allowed to prove by parol evidence the latter agreement if objected to? Give reasons.

A.—In a contract of this kind, which is required by law to be in writing, a party cannot come forward as plaintiff to claim the performance of the real agreement which is not completely expressed by the written contract. But parol evidence of the oral variation of the written contract will be available for the defendant in an action for specific performance. *Townsend* v. *Strangroon, 6 Ves, 328,* affords the best illustration. There were cross suits, one for specific performance of the written agreement as varied by an oral agreement, the other for specific performance of the written agreement without the variation. The fact of parol variations from the written agreement being established both suits were dismissed. The result of a plaintiff attempting to enforce an agreement with alleged parol variations, if the defendant disproves the variations and chooses to abide by the written agreement, may be a decree for the specific performance of the agreement as it stands at the plaintiff's costs. But it is open for a plaintiff to admit a parol addition or variation made for the defendant's benefit, and so enforce specific performance, which the defendant might have successfully resisted if it had been sought to enforce the written agreement simply.

Pollock, p. 509.

21. Q.—What are the three general grounds on which contracts may be held illegal by the Common Law?

A.—Contracts are at Common Law illegal when they are contrary to (1) Positive Law, (2) Morality, and (3) Public Policy.

22. Q.—Will a promise to pay a sum of money be valid and binding if the consideration for it is (a) a mere moral consideration, (b) a debt barred by the Statute of Limitations? Give reason of the difference, if any.

A.—(a) "A mere moral obligation arising from a past benefit not conferred at the request of the defendant" is not a good consideration, as decided in 1840 in *Eastwood* v. *Kenyon*.

Pollock, p. 232.

(b) An apparently exceptional case to this rule is the acknowledgment of barred debts. The theory is that the legal remedy is lost but the debt is not destroyed, and the debt subsisting in this dormant condition is a good consideration for a new promise to pay it. Or the debtor may wave his protection under the Statute if he deliberately chooses to do so.

Pollock, pp. 233-4 and 631-2.

23. Q.—State briefly in what respects simple contracts are inferior to contracts by deed.

A.—A contract by deed is good for twenty years whilst a simple contract is only good for six years.

In a contract by deed consideration is presumed by the formalities, but in a simple contract consideration must be proven. A contract by deed proves itself by production.

24. Q.—If one of two joint makers of a promissory note give a mortgage to the holder to secure the amount of the note, will such mortgage have any effect by way of merger of the note ? Why ?

A.—No. A merger will not take place unless the parties giving the mortgage are the same as the makers of the joint note.

25. Q.—Under the 4th Section of the Statute of Frauds, will a man's verbal promise to marry a woman be binding on him ? Reasons.

A.—The verbal promise to marry is binding on him.

A promise to marry does not come under the 4th Section of the Statute of Frauds, the consideration being not marriage, but the other parties reciprocal promise to marry, and therefore it is not required to be in writing in order to be valid ; but an agreement in consideration of marriage is within the 4th Section, and must be in writing in order to be valid.

Pollock, p. 223.

26. Q.—What is the difference between a breach of a

condition precedent and a breach of warranty on the part of the vendor of goods as regards the remedy of the vendee therefor?

A.—A breach of a condition precedent justifies a repudiation of the contract. A breach of warranty gives rise to a claim for damages.

Benjamin, p. 546.

27. Q.—Where a purchaser has been induced to enter into a contract of purchase by the fraudulent misrepresentation of the agent of an innocent vendor, what remedy has he, and against whom?

A.—The purchaser can maintain an action of deceit against the innocent principal where the fraud of the agent has been committed within the scope of his authority, and where the principal has been benefitted by it. And the purchaser also has an action against the agent who is liable for his fraudulent act.

28. Q.—What is the difference between a public sale and a private sale, as regards the authority of the auctioneer to sign the memorandum of the sale, as agent for the parties, under the Statute of Frauds?

A.—The auctioneer is the agent of both parties to sign the memorandum at the public sale, but is only the agent of the vendor at a private sale.

Benjamin, pp. 234 and 235.

29. Q.—Define briefly the right of *stoppage in transitu*, and explain the effect which the exercise of such right has upon the contract of sale and the title to the goods.

A.—It is the right of the vendor to stop the goods while they are in course of transit to the vendee, in the event of the vendee becoming insolvent. The right only arises on the *insolvency* of the buyer. The effect of this remedy of the vendor is simply to restore the goods to his *possession*, so as to enable him to exercise his rights as an unpaid vendor, but not to rescind the sale.

Benjamin, pp. 817 and 866.

30. Q.—If a tailor makes a suit of clothes to order supplying the material himself, and delivers the clothes to his customer, will his claim, in case of being obliged to sue for his pay, be only for goods sold and delivered, or for work done and materials provided, and why?

A.—The action must be for goods sold and delivered. In 1861 it was decided in *Lee* v. *Griffin*, "that if the contract is intended to result in transferring for a price from B. to A., a chattel in which A. had no previous property, it is a contract for the sale of a chattel."

Benjamin, pp. 90 *et seq.*

31. Q.—A. orders from B., a liquor dealer, one doz. ale; B. sends two doz. bottles of ale. Has A. a right (*a*) to return the whole two doz.; (*b*) to keep one doz. and return the rest; (*c*) to keep a half doz. and return the rest? Reasons.

A.—(*a*) Yes. (*b*) Yes. (*c*) Yes. A. orders one doz. and B. sends two doz., but does not thereby comply with the terms of the order. Therefore the sending of the two doz. will amount to a new proposal, and A. may send all back, or he may retain as many as he chooses and send back the balance, and he will then be liable only for the price of those retained, as this will be a new contract.

Benjamin, p. 55.

32. Q.—A written contract of sale of goods worth over $40 is silent in regard to price. Will oral evidence in respect to price be admissible in an action on the contract ? If so, for what purpose ? Give reasons.

A.—Yes, oral evidence is admissible for the purpose of ascertaining what is a reasonable price. " It is only necessary that the price should be mentioned in the memorandum where the price is one of the ingredients of the bargain . . . and it is admitted on all hands that if a *specific* price is agreed on, and that price is omitted in the writing, the memorandum is insufficient."

Benjamin, pp. 214 *et seq.*

33. Q.—Where a chattel is to be made to the order of a purchaser, what warranty, if any, is implied by law ?

A.—Where a chattel is made to order, there is an implied warranty that it is reasonably fit for the purpose for which it is ordinarily used, or that it is fit for the special purpose intended by the buyer, if that purpose be communicated at the time the order is given.

Benjamin, p. 684.

34. Q.—Will a tender be good (a) if accompanied by a protest that the sum tendered is more than is due (b) if the sum is tendered expressly " as the amount of your bill " ?

A.—(a) A tender accompanied by a protest that the amount is not due is a good tender. *Scott* v. *Uxbridge Railway Company.* (b) And where the defendant produced the money, saying, " I am come with the amount of your bill," the tender was held unconditional and good. *Henwood* v. *Oliver.*

Benjamin, pp. 711 and 712.

35. Q.—Will the transfer of a bill of lading to an indorsee for value who knows the price is not paid prevent the vendor from stopping the goods *in transitu*? Why?

A.—Yes, because a man may be perfectly honest in dealing for goods which he knows have not been paid for. As long as the endorsee acts *bona fide* it does not signify whether he knows the price is unpaid or not, and the endorsation will defeat the vendor's right to *stoppage in transitu*.

Benjamin, p. 864.

36. Q.—A. by a verbal bargain sells to B. one hundred bushels of barley at fifty cents per bushel by sample. The barley is sent to B., who at once returns it with the following note, signed by himself and addressed to A.: "Dear Sir,—The hundred bushels of barley which I bought from you at fifty cents per bushel I refuse to accept, and return as not according to sample. B." In fact the barley is according to sample. Can A. maintain an action against B.? Reasons.

A.—Yes, A. can maintain an action against B. A letter repudiating the contract may be so worded as to furnish a sufficient note of the bargain to satisfy the 17th section of the Statute of Frauds.

Benjamin, p. 218.

37. Q.—A. voluntarily pays a debt which B. owes to C. Subsequently B. promises to pay A. the amount. Can A. recover the amount from B. on this promise? Why?

A.—Yes. The law implies a previous request which is necessary to support the promise to pay.

38. Q.—What is the presumption of law in regard to the wife's authority to bind her husband for the price of necessaries, (a) when they are living together, (b) when they are living apart?

A.—(a) When they are living together the wife is presumed to be the husband's agent, but this presumption may be rebutted. (b) When they are living apart the wife is presumed not to be the husband's agent.

39. Q.—A dentist verbally agrees to make and supply a set of artificial teeth for $75. Is such a contract binding under the Statute of Frauds? Why?

A.—This is a contract for the sale of a chattel and is therefore not binding under the Statute. This was the decision in *Lee* v. *Griffin, 30 L. J. Q. B. 252*, and it has been followed in Ontario by *Wolfenden* v. *Wilson, 33 Up. Can. Q. B. 442.* If the price had been less than $40, the contract would have been binding under the Statute.

Benjamin, p. 98.

40. Q.—A. purchases from B. by verbal agreement an elm tree growing on his land. The tree is to be cut down and converted into cordwood by B. and then delivered to A., who is then to pay for the same at $3.00 per cord. The tree contains five cords of wood and its value $15. Is the contract binding under the Statute of Frauds? Reasons.

A.—This is an executory agreement for the sale of goods to be severed from the land, and the property is to be transferred after the thing is severed. It does not come within the 4th section of the Statute of Frauds since it is not an interest in land, nor does it come within the 17th section for the value of the wood is less than $40.00, and the contract is therefore binding.

When the agreement is that the property is to be transferred before the thing is severed, it seems clear enough that it is *not* a contract for the sale of goods ; it is a contract for a sale, but the thing to be sold is not goods.   The true subject of enquiry in each case is, when do the parties intend that the property is to pass ?

.   Benjamin, pp. 108 and 109.

41. Q.—In case of a sale of goods on trial what effect has the mere failure to return the goods within the time specified for trial ?

A.—If the goods are not returned within the time specified for trial the sale becomes absolute.

Benjamin, p. 591.

42. Q.—A purchaser buys according to sample twenty barrels of " refined American coal oil."   The oil delivered corresponds with the sample but is Canadian oil.   Is the purchaser bound to accept it ?

A.—The purchaser is not bound to accept it because it does not answer the description.

43. Q.—A man sells a boat to another knowing at the time that the boat is being bought for the special purpose of being used in smuggling.   Can the vendor recover the price by an action ?

A.—No ; because the contract is for an illegal purpose.
Benjamin, p. 497.

If the vendor were a foreigner then compare Question No. 3 *ante.*

44. Q.—A merchant in Newmarket buys goods on credit from a wholesale merchant in Toronto and sends his servant for them with a wagon. The vendor delivers the goods to the servant, who starts for Newmarket, and then discovers that the purchaser is insolvent. Can he stop the goods *in transitu* before they arrive at Newmarket and take them from the servant ?

A.—No. The delivery to the servant amounts to delivery to the master, and the goods are in the actual possession of the master the moment his servant gets them.

Benjamin, p. 828.

45. Q.—What is the law as to the person from whom and the person to whom the consideration for a simple contract must pass ?

A.—The consideration must pass *from* the promisee *to* the promissor.

46 Q.—If goods are sold and delivered on Sunday and are afterwards kept by the purchaser without any offer to return them, can the price be recovered in an action at law ?

A.—No ; but if he keeps the goods and afterwards makes a promise to pay for them he is then liable for the price of the goods retained.

Benjamin, pp. 539 and 540.

47. Q.—What is the law as to the liability of the principal on a contract made by his agent, who at the time of making it informs the other party that he is acting as agent but does not name his principal?

A.—*Prima facie* there is a contract with the agent, but on discovering the principal the third party may elect to

Q.A.—4

proceed against the principal. But the right of the third
party to hold the principal liable is subject to the qualifica-
tion that the state of the account between the principal and
the agent must not be altered to the prejudice of the principal. But this doctrine has been disapproved by the
Court of Appeal as going too far. The principal is discharged as against the other party by payment to his own
agent, only, if that party has by his conduct led the principal to believe that he has settled with the agent, or,
perhaps, if the principal has in good faith paid the agent at
a time when the other party still gave credit to the agent
alone, and would naturally, from some peculiar character
of the business or otherwise, be supposed by the principal
to do so. Again, the other party may choose to give credit
to the agent exclusively after discovering the principal, and
in this case he cannot afterwards hold the principal liable ;
and statements or conduct of the party, which lead the
principal to believe that the agent only will be held liable,
and on the faith of which the agent acts, will have the
same result. And although the party may elect to sue the
principal, yet he must make such election within a reasonable time after discovering him.

Pollock, pp. 169 and 170.

48. Q.—Goods are sold in Montreal to be delivered in
Toronto. When delivered to the railway company they are
in good order, but on the way become unavoidably deteriorated by the conveyance. Must the loss be borne by the
vendor or vendee ? Why ?

A.—The loss must be borne by the vendee, because the
vendor delivered the goods to the carrier in good condition
and was thus relieved of further responsibility.

Bull v. *Robinson*.
Benjamin, p. 687.

49. Q.—What is the difference between a lease and an agreement for a lease, as regards the necessity for a writing?

A.—A lease for more than three years, or reserving a rent less than two-thirds of the improved value, must be in writing and now by deed. But an informal lease, though void as a lease, may be good as an agreement for a lease.

Pollock, p. 224.

An *agreement for a lease* must be in writing though it need not be by deed ; but *all leases* (except those for more than three years or reserving a rent less than two-thirds of the improved value) may be verbal.

50. Q.—How far does delivery of goods to a carrier go towards constituting an *acceptance and receipt* to satisfy the Statute of Frauds ?

A.—The delivery of goods to a carrier is not an *acceptance and receipt* by the vendee. It is a delivery of the goods to the vendee and amounts to a *receipt* but not an *acceptance*. (Compare question No. 4, *ante.*)

Benjamin, pp. 142 *et seq.*

But, however, acceptance may precede the actual receipt, as where the vendee has inspected and approved of the specific goods at or before the time of purchasing.

51. Q.—A. sells to B. for $30 a stack of hay standing on A.'s farm. The hay is to remain where it is for three months and is to be paid for before removal. Before the three months expire and before removal or payment the hay is burnt without the fault of any one. Who bears the loss and why ?

A.—The question to be considered here is whether the property has passed or not. This is the sale of a specific chattel and nothing remains to be done by the vendor.

In *Tarling* v. *Baxter L. J. Q. B. 148*, the facts were the same as in this case, and it was held to be an immediate, not a prospective sale, although the hay was not to be cut till paid for. Bayley, J., said:—"The rule of law is that where there is an immediate sale and nothing remains to be done by the vendor as between him and the vendee, *the property in the thing sold vests in the vendee.*" This case was followed in *Martindale* v. *Smith*, 1 *Q. B. 389*, in 1841.

In the case in question, therefore, the property in the stack of hay passed to B. at the time of the sale, and he must bear the loss. However, it is always important to ascertain what was the intention of the parties as to the passing of the property, and if it be shown that it was clearly their intention that the property should not pass, or that the buyer should not assume the risk before the property had vested in him, then the decision should be otherwise.

Benjamin, p. 267.

52. Q.—Explain briefly the difference between a condition precedent and a warranty, and show in what way the former may be changed into the latter by the conduct of the vendee.

A.—See question No. 26, *ante*.

Though a man may refuse to perform his promise until the other party has complied with a *condition precedent*, yet, if he has received and accepted a substantial part of that which was to be performed in his favor, the *condition precedent* changes its character and becomes a *warranty*, or an independent agreement affording no defence to an action but giving a right to a counter-claim for damages.

Benjamin, p. 549.

53. Q.—Goods which have been sold remain in possession of the vendor. The vendee having made default in payment of the price the vendor re-sells the goods. Is he liable to an action by the vendee? If so, in what way and for what amount?

A.—The vendor is liable to an action for damages. But only the actual damage can be recovered, *i.e.*, the difference between the contract price and the market value on the re-sale; if there be no proof of such difference the recovery will be for nominal damages only. When the vendor has a right to sell on default, then of course no action would lie at the suit of the vendee against him.

Benjamin, p. 780.

54. Q.—Do the following agreements require to be in writing under the Statute of Frauds: (*a*) An agreement to pay a person a sum of money on the day of his marriage, (*b*) an agreement of hiring for a term of three years with liberty to either party to terminate the hiring by one month's notice? Give reasons.

A.—(*a*) The Statute says: "Any agreement made upon consideration of marriage must be in writing." If this agreement is in consideration of marriage it must be in writing, but if the consideration is otherwise, then the Statute says: "It must be in writing if it is not to be performed within the space of one year from the making thereof." The wording of this clause is "is not to be," not "is not," or "may not be." This means an agreement that on the face of it cannot be performed within a year. An agreement capable of being performed within a year, and not showing any intention to put off the performance till after a year, is not within this clause. Hence, an agreement to pay a person a sum of money on the day of his marriage need not be in writing, as it may be performed within a year. (b) But an agreement is not excluded from the operation of the clause by being made determinable on a contingency that may happen within a year.

Pollock, pp. 223 and 224.

55. Q.—On a dissolution of partnership between two solicitors practising in Toronto, the retiring partner covenants never to practise in Toronto or at any place within two thousand miles thereof. Would this covenant be of any effect? If so, what? Reasons.

A.—No, the covenant would not be of any effect. In contracts of this nature the *restraint* must be reasonable, and in this case it is not within reasonable limits either as to time or space, and therefore the covenant is not to be enforced.

Pollock, pp. 362 *et seq*.

56. Q.—When a statute imposes a penalty upon any one entering into a particular kind of contract, but does not expressly prohibit or declare such contract ⸺ illegal, has it any, and if so what, effect upon the ⸺ ⸺ ty of the con- tract, and why?

A.—A penalty *prima facie* imports a prohibition. A party could not be permitted to sue on a contract where the whole subject matter was in direct violation of the provisions of an Act of Parliament. In *Bensley v. Bignold* a printer could not recover for his work or materials where he had omitted to print his name on the work printed, as then required by Statute.

Pollock, p. 309.

57. Q.—A written offer for the purchase of goods, for the price of $100, containing all the terms of the purchase, is signed by the purchaser and verbally accepted by the vendor. Is such contract binding (*a*) on the vendor, (*b*) on the vendee? Reasons.

A.—The memorandum is sufficient, if a mere signed proposal, when it is supplemented by parol proof of acceptance.
Benjamin, p. 218.

(*a*) It is not binding on the vendor because he did not sign the memorandum.

(*b*) It is binding on the vendee because he signed the memorandum.

The contract is good or not good at the election of the party who has not signed the memorandum.
Benjamin, p. 219.

58. Q.—In France a promissory note is void unless it is stamped and an action must be brought on it within five years from maturity. An action is brought in Ontario against a person residing here on a note made and payable in France. Two grounds of defence are pleaded : (*a*) that the note was not duly stamped under the law of France ; (*b*) that the action was not commenced within five years from the maturity of the note as required by the law of France. Do these grounds form a good defence? Reasons.

A.—(*a*) This is a good defence to the action. If it had been a rule of local procedure it would not be admitted as a defence, but, as the French Law makes the stamp necessary to the validity of the instrument, that is a condition precedent to its having any legal effect at all.
Pollock, p. 337.

(b) This is not a good defence to the action. The Law of Limitations does not relate to the substance of the cause of action, but to the procedure, and these enactments belong to the *lex fori* and not to the *lex contractus.*

Pollock, p. 633.

59. Q.—What *warranty* and what *condition* does the law imply in every sale of goods by sample ?

A.—In every sale of goods by sample the law implies a *warranty* that the quality of the bulk is equal to the sample.

Benjamin, p. 636.

And the law implies a *condition* that the buyer shall have a fair opportunity to compare the bulk with the sample.

Benjamin, p. 590.

60. Q.—A Toronto merchant gives a verbal order to a Montreal merchant for 100 tons of oil at $5 per ton. The oil is delivered by the vendor to the G. T. R. Co. in Montreal, and while being carried on the railway to Toronto is destroyed by the act of God. Who bears the loss, and why ?

A.—The loss must be borne by the vendor. This is a verbal order, and the delivery to the carrier constitutes a receipt but not an acceptance by the vendee, and the property in the goods did not pass.

Where a vendor delivers goods to a carrier on a written order of the vendee, then the appropriation is determined and the property vests at once.

In all these cases the general rule is that the intention of the parties determines when the property passes ; acts which would be held to amount to a transfer of the pro-

perty will not have that effect if the intention of the
parties to the contrary be apparent from the contract; and
the various rules which are laid down in regard to the
passing of the property do not, therefore, hold good when
an intention at variance with them can be deduced from
the words or acts of the parties.

Smith's Mercantile Law, pp. 603-605.

Benjamin, p. 305.

61. Q.—Explain briefly the difference between a contract
of sale of a specific article, and a contract of sale of unascertained chattels in regard to its effect in passing the title
to the buyer.

A.—In the sale of specific articles the property passes
immediately even though the vendor retains the possession.

Benjamin, p. 263.

But where the goods are to be weighed, measured or
tested, the property does not pass until this is done.

Benjamin, p. 268.

62. Q.—What is the difference between a voluntary and
a compulsory payment by one man of another man's debt
in regard to his right to recover the amount from the
debtor? Explain fully the reason of your answer.

A.—If one man *voluntarily* pays a debt, which another
man was legally bound to pay, he will not thereby acquire
a right to recover the amount from the debtor; but if the
debtor afterwards promises to pay the debt the law will
imply a previous request necessary to support the promise.

Pollock, p. 238.

If one man is *compelled* to pay a debt which another
man was legally bound to pay, he will thereby acquire a

right to recover the amount from the debtor. A good
example of this is the ordinary case of a surety, who, if he
is compelled to pay, can recover the amount from the
original debtor.

63. Q.—A. in consideration of valuable services, which
have been rendered to him by B., agrees with B. to pay
B.'s son C. $1,000. Can C. recover the money from A. ?
Why?

A.—C. cannot recover the money because he is not a
party to the contract. No third person can become entitled
by the contract itself to demand the performance of any
duty under the contract. But as an exception to this we
find that " Provisions contained in a settlement made upon
and in consideration of marriage for the benefit of children
to be born of the marriage, or, in the case of a woman
marrying again, for the benefit of her children by any
former marriage, may be enforced by the persons entitled
to the benefit thereof."

Pollock, p. 249.

It was for a long time not fully settled whether a contract between A. and B. that one of them should do something for the benefit of C., did or did not give C. a right of
action on the contract. And there was positive authority
that at all events a contract made for the benefit of a
person nearly related to one or both of the contracting
parties might be enforced by that person. However, the
rule is now distinctly established that a third person cannot
sue on a contract made by others for his benefit, even if the
contracting parties have agreed that he may, and that near
relationship makes no difference as regards any common
law right of action. This was decided by the Court of

Queen's Bench in *Tweedle* v. *Atkinson, 1 B. & S. 393, 30 L. J. Q. B. 265.*

Pollock, pp. 260 and 261.

64. Q.—In what different ways can a vendor's lien for the price of goods sold be waived or lost ?

A.—The vendor's lien may be waived when the contract is formed, or it may be abandoned afterwards. It may be waived by a sale on credit, unless there is a special agreement to the contrary or proof of usage in the particular trade. It may be waived by taking a bill of exchange or other security. It may be abandoned by the delivery of the goods to the buyer, and, where the vendor permits the buyer to exercise acts of ownership on goods lying on the premises of a third person not a bailee of the vendor, his lien will be lost.

Benjamin, pp. 781 *et seq.*

65. Q.—In cases of executed consideration when will the law imply a previous *request* necessary to support a promise and when will it imply both the *request* and the *promise ?*

A.—The law would imply a previous *request* when a man does that which another was compellable to do, and the latter afterwards promises to pay. The law will imply both a *request* and a *promise :* (1) When a man is compelled to do that which another is liable to do, or (2) when one man makes use or derives some benefit from some voluntary act or labor of another.

66. Q.—When a vendor delivers goods to a common carrier to be conveyed to the purchaser is the carrier as a general rule the bailee of the vendor or of the purchaser ?

A.—The carrier as a general rule is the bailee of the purchaser.

Benjamin, p. 687.

67. Q.—When may a party rescind a contract of sale on the ground that he has been induced to enter into it by an innocent representation not amounting to a *warranty?*

A.—The contract may be rescinded : (1) When the representation is part of the promise or a term of the contract ; (2) when the contract is made conditional on the truth of the representation, *i.e.*, when they mean to contract only on the footing of its being true ; and (3) when material representations are made in contracts *uberrimae fidei*, and they turn out to be untrue even though innocently made.

Warranty is distinguished as being a distinct collateral agreement that a representation shall be true so that its untruth shall in no case avoid the contract but shall be matter for compensation.

Pollock, p. 525.

68. Q.—Define *fructus industriales* and *fructus naturales* and explain the difference between them as regards the application of the Statute of Frauds ?

A.—*Fructus industriales* are chattels, and an agreement for the sale of them, whether mature or immature, whether the property in them is transferred *before* or *after severance*, is not an agreement for the sale of an interest in land, and is not governed by the 4th section of the Statute of Frauds.

Fructus naturales are part of the soil *before severance*, and an agreement, therefore, vesting an interest in them in the purchaser before severance, is governed by the 4th section ; but if the interest is not to be vested till they are converted

ee of the

of sale on
o it by an
anty !
the repre-
contract ;
e truth of
tract only
material
fidei, and
y made.
collateral
so that its
it shall be

s *naturales*
egards the

agreement
re, whether
r *severance,*
st in land,
Statute of

erance, and
:hem in the
th section ;
e converted

into chattels by severance, then the agreement is an executory agreement for the sale of goods, wares and merchandise, governed by the 17th and not by the 4th section of the Statute of Frauds.

Benjamin, p. 116.

69. Q.—When may several separate writings, only one of which is signed, be read together as constituting an agreement or memorandum thereof under the Statute of Frauds ?

A.—Where the memorandum of the bargain between the parties is contained in separate pieces of paper, and where these papers contain the *whole* bargain, they form together such a memorandum as will satisfy the Statute of Frauds, provided the contents of the signed paper make such reference to the other written paper or papers, as to enable the Court to construe the whole of them together as constituting all the terms of the bargain. And the same result will follow if the other papers were attached or fastened to the signed paper *at the time of the signature.*

But if it be necessary to adduce parol evidence, in order to connect a signed paper with others unsigned, by reason of the absence of any internal evidence in the contents of the signed paper to show a reference to, or connection with, the unsigned papers, then the several papers taken together do not constitute a memorandum *in writing* of the bargain so as to satisfy the Statute of Frauds.

Benjamin, p. 185.

70. Q.—When will and when will not a vendor be deprived of his right of *stoppage in transitu* by having taken a bill or note for the price of the goods ?

A.—A vendor will be deprived of his right to *stoppage in transitu* if he takes bills or securities in *absolute* payment. He must in such cases seek his remedy on the securities, having no further right on the goods.

But if a vendor takes bills or securities as *conditional* payment, even though he may have negotiated the bills so that they are outstanding in third hands unmatured, he will not thereby be deprived of his right to *stoppage in transitu*.

Benjamin, p. 822.

71. Q.—What warranties are implied by law (*a*) on the sale of an engine manufactured by the vendor for the vendee, (*b*) on the sale of goods by description which have not been examined by the vendee ?

A.—(*a*) See Question No. 33 *ante*.

(*b*) On the sale of a chattel, as being of a particular description, there is an implied condition that the article is of that description and a warranty that it is merchantable.

Benjamin, p. 635.

72. Q.—A Montreal merchant sells goods to a Toronto merchant and agrees to deliver them in Toronto. Which of them must bear the loss occasioned by the usual and necessary deterioration of the goods by their carriage on the railway ?

A.—If the vendor sells goods undertaking to make the delivery himself at a distant place, he thus assumes the risk of carriage and the carrier is the vendor's agent. But the vendor's duty to deliver them in merchantable condition is complied with if the goods are in proper condition when delivered to *the carrier*, provided the injury received during the transit does not exceed that which must necessarily result from the transit. In *Bull* v. *Robinson, 10 Ex. 342; 24 L. J. Ex. 165,* hoop-iron was sold in Staffordshire, deliverable in Liverpool in the winter, and the vendor was held to have made a good delivery, although the iron was rusted and unmerchantable when delivered in Liverpool, on proof that this deterioriation was the necessary result of the transit, and that the iron was bright and in good order when it left Staffordshire.

Therefore in this case the Toronto merchant must bear the loss.

> Benjamin, p. 687.

73. Q.—Is a verbal agreement to marry binding, or must an agreement to marry be in writing, in order to satisfy the Statute of Frauds, which requires any agreement made in consideration of marriage to be evidenced by writing? Reasons.

A.—A promise to marry does not come within the Statute of Frauds, and need not be in writing, the consideration being not marriage but the other party's reciprocal promise to marry.

> Pollock, p. 223.

74. Q.—When a person making an offer of sale accompanies it with a promise to leave the offer open for a certain length of time, what are his rights in regard to retracting the offer within that time? Reasons.

A.—A promise to give time to consider an offer is without consideration, and does not constitute a contract. The person making the offer of sale may revoke it at any time before acceptance.

> Pollock, p. 99.

75. Q.—What will be the effect, if any, upon the passing of the property in goods sold (*a*) if by the agreement something is to be done to the goods by the vendor in order to put them into a deliverable state, (*b*) if, by the agreement, something is to be done to the goods by the vendor after delivery?

A.—(*a*) If something is to be done to the goods by the vendor in order to put them into a deliverable state the property will not pass until this has been done.

Benjamin, p. 268.

(*b*) If something is to be done to the goods by the vendor after the delivery the property in the goods will pass notwithstanding this; as where, by a custom of trade, goods continue to lie at a wharf after sale, and the vendor was bound to pay for warehousing, the property in the goods sold had nevertheless passed; or, as where a vendor of a watch agrees to keep it in good running order, the property in the watch passes on delivery.

Benjamin, 275 and 276.

76. Q.—Explain briefly what is meant by a reservation of the *jus disponendi* on a sale of goods.

A.—The reservation of the *jus disponendi* is the vendor's purpose to retain the ownership in the goods until he is paid.

Benjamin, pp. 328 *et seq.*

Also read the eight principles which have been established by the numerous authorities on this subject as found in

Benjamin, pp. 352 *et seq.*

77. Q.—In what case must a contract be founded on a consideration, even though made by deed?

A.—The contracts which require consideration even though made by deed are, (1) contracts in restraint of trade, (2) a covenant to stand seized, and (3) a conveyance under the Statute of Uses.

78. Q.—What is the difference in point of validity between an agreement for a future separation of husband and wife, and an agreement providing a fund for the wife's support on the occasion of an immediate separation ; and what is the reason of such difference ?

A.—A contract providing for and fixing the terms of an *immediate separation* is good ; but a contract for a *future separation* is held to be void, because the law considers that such a contract would be against public policy, and will not permit anything which might have the effect of preventing a reconciliation between the parties, in case they might wish to change their minds before the time agreed upon for the future separation.

79. Q.—What promise does the law imply on the part of a *remunerated* and *unremunerated* agent respectively ?

A.—In the case of a *remunerated* agent the law implies a promise by the agent that he will use all possible care and diligence in the discharge of his duties ; but an *unremunerated* agent, who has actually entered on the performance of his duties, is only liable for his negligence. For further information on this subject read the celebrated case of *Coggs* v. *Bernard, Ld. Raym. 909.*

Broom, pp. 749, 883 *et seq.*

80. Q.—What is the effect of a written contract of purchase of goods being entered into by a party as agent for a non-existent principal ?

Q. A.—5

A.—The party is *primâ facie* personally liable in his character of agent. And even if the contract is so framed as to exclude that liability (and therefore any correlative right to sue), he is not precluded from showing that he himself is the principal and suing in that character.

Pollock, p. 176.

81. Q.— A particular horse is sold for a stated price to be delivered at a future day. Before the time for delivery arrives the horse without any fault of the vendor dies. What are the rights and liabilities of the parties respectively as to delivery and payment ? Reasons.

A.—The <u>vendor is excused from performing his contract to deliver and the vendee is excused from payment</u>.

In *Taylor* v. *Caldwell, 3 B. and S. 826, 32 L.J.Q.B. 164.* the Court laid down the following principle :—"Where from the nature of the contract it appears that the parties must from the beginning have known that it could not be fulfilled unless, when the time for the fulfilment of the contract arrived, some particular specified thing continued to exist, so that when entering into the contract they must have contemplated such continued existence as the foundation of what was to be done ; there, in the absence of any express or implied warranty that the thing shall exist, the contract is not to be considered a positive contract, but subject to the implied condition that the parties shall be excused in case, before breach, performance becomes impossible from the perishing of the thing without default of the contractor."

Pollock, pp. 414 and 415.

82. Q.—Is it necessary to the validity of a delivery of a deed as an escrow ; (a) that it should be expressed in

words to be an escrow; (b) that it should be delivered to some person other than the grantee?

A.—(a) It is not necessary to express in words that it is an escrow, (b) but it should be delivered to some third person, to be delivered by him as the act and deed of the grantor, when certain specified conditions shall be performed.

But later cases show that it may now be delivered even to the grantee to take effect on certain conditions.

83. Q.—Is parol evidence admissible (a) to show that a written contract has omitted a material term of the bargain, (b) to show that an additional term was verbally agreed to after the written contract was made?

A.—(a) Parol evidence is not admissible to vary a written contract, but it is admitted to show that a written contract has omitted a material term of the bargain.

(b) Parol evidence that an additional term was verbally agreed to after the written contract was made is admissible as a defence to an action for specific performance of the written agreement, but it is not admissible to obtain specific performance of the agreement as varied by the subsequent verbal agreement.

Pollock, pp. 508 and 509.

84. Q—Explain the difference as regards the passing of the title between a sale of a specific chattel and a sale of unascertained goods?

A.—A specific chattel passes at once as soon as it is appropriated to the vendee.

Benjamin, pp. 265-267.

Unascertained goods do not pass until they are weighed, measured, or in some other way ascertained.

Benjamin, p. 268.

85. Q.—In what ways may a sale on trial become an absolute sale?

A.—If the goods are kept beyond the time for trial the sale becomes absolute.

Benjamin, p. 590.

86. Q.—What is the test by which it may be determined whether an affirmation made by the vendor of goods at the time of sale is or is not a warranty?

A.—The test is whether the vendor assumes to assert a fact of which the buyer is ignorant, or merely states an opinion or judgment upon a matter of which the vendor has no special knowledge, and on which the buyer may be expected also to have an opinion and to exercise his judgment.

Benjamin, p. 608.

87. Q.—Are the following tenders good: (a) A debtor owing $90.00 hands his creditor ten ten-dollar bank bills and tells him to take out of them what is due him. (b) The debtor hands the creditor five twenty-dollar bank bills and demands the change?

A.—(a) This is not a good tender since the bank bills are not *legal* tender, but otherwise it is good.

Becans v. Rees, 5 M. & W. 306.

(b) This is not a good tender.

Watkins v. Robb, 2 Esp. 711.

Benjamin, p. 705.

88. Q.—What is in general the consideration for a sale of goods; the payment of the price, or the purchaser's obligation to pay it ?

A.—The consideration for the sale of goods is in general the purchaser's *obligation* to pay the price and not the payment of the price itself.

89. Q.—If the amount written on the body of the note and the figures in the margin do not agree will oral evidence be admitted to prove which is right ?

A.—No. It is laid down that in such a case the amount written in the body of the note must govern.

90. Q.—An agreement is made verbally between A. B. and C. for good and sufficient consideration, by which A. assumes and agrees to pay a debt owing by B. to C., and C. releases B. from the debt. Is such agreement valid ? Why ?

A.—The Statute of Frauds enacts that : "Any special promise to answer for the debt, default or miscarriage of another person must be evidenced by some written agreement or memorandum or note signed by the party to be charged or his agent."

This agreement in question does not come within the Statute and is therefore valid. This is not a guarantee because A. promises to be primarily liable and B. is discharged. The statute does not invalidate one's oral promises to pay his own debt though in a form which will work the discharge of another.

Pollock, p. 222.

91. Q.—In what three classes are all contracts divided by the Common Law of England ?

A.—(1) *Contracts of Record*, as :—Judgments, Recogni-
   zances, and Statutes Staple.

   (2) *Specialties*, as :—Deeds and bonds being under
   seal.

   (8) *Simple Contracts*, as :—Verbal or written contracts not under seal.

There is no distinct class of *written* contracts.

92. Q.—What is the general rule of law as to the right
of a man to maintain an action to recover back money paid
by him in pursuance of an illegal contract, and what exceptions are there to the rule ?

A.—The general rule is that he cannot recover, but,
where the unlawful agreement is executory only, the money
or the goods may be recovered.

In *Taylor* v. *Bowers, 1 Q. B. D. 291, C. A.*, Mellish, L. J.,
said : "If money is paid, or goods delivered, for an illegal
purpose, the person who had so paid the money or delivered
the goods may recover them back before the illegal purpose
is carried out; but if he waits till the illegal purpose is
carried out, or if he seeks to enforce the illegal transaction, in neither case can he maintain an action."

Benjamin, p. 497.

93. Q.—What is the duty of the vendor in regard to
delivery of goods where the contract is silent as to delivery ?

A.—In the absence of a contrary agreement the vendor
is not bound to send or carry the goods to the vendee.
He does all that he is bound to do by leaving or placing
the goods at the buyer's disposal, so that the latter may
remove them without lawful obstruction.

Benjamin, p. 671.

94. Q.—When the vendor has agreed to send the goods sold, but no time for sending them has been mentioned, within what time must he send them ?

A.—Where the vendor has agreed to send the goods, and nothing is said as to time, he must send within a *reasonable time*; and when the sale is in writing, if nothing is said as to time, parol evidence is admissible of the facts and circumstances attending the sale in order to determine what is a reasonable time.

Benjamin, p. 674.

95. Q.—How may a vendee extinguish the vendor's right of *stoppage in transitu* before the transitus is ended ?

A.—The right to *stoppage in transitu* is only defensible when a bill of lading, or other document of title representing the goods, has been transferred to a *bona fide* endorsee for value.

Benjamin, p. 856.

———————

(N.B.—From this collection on contracts and sales there have been excluded forty-six questions which were repetitions.—F. L. W.)

CHAPTER III.

EQUITY.

1. Q.—Distinguish between the doctrines of common law and of equity with respect to the assignment of choses in action, and illustrate the distinction by an example.

A.—Formerly at common law, as Lord Coke said, " No possibility, right, title nor thing in action could be granted or assigned to strangers ; for that would be the occasion of multiplying of contentions and suits, of great oppression of the people, and the subversion of the due and equal execution of justice," but, in equity, the reasons given by Lord Coke have been wholly disregarded, and assignments for valuable consideration have been held valid, upon the same principle that equity enforces the performance of agreements when such agreements are for value, and of course are not contrary to its own rules or to public policy.

A mere expectancy, therefore, as that of an heir-at-law to the estate of his ancestor ; or the interest which a person may take under the will of another, who is living, is assignable in equity for valuable consideration.

Snell, pp. 90 and 91.

2. Q.—A. assaults B. under circumstances which give B. a right of action against A. in respect thereof. B. assigns his right of action to C., who commences an action thereon, which is defended by A., who asserts that the cause of action is not assignable. Is this a good defence ? Give reasons.

A.—Equity will not enforce the assignment of a mere naked right to litigate, *i.e.*, of a right which, from its very nature, is incapable of conferring any benefit except through the medium of a suit.

The reason of this is founded on the principle that equity will not give any encouragement to litigation.

Snell, p. 99.

3. Q.—A testator devises certain lands to a trustee upon trust to sell the same and pay certain debts and legacies, and to pay over the balance of the proceeds to such of the students-at-law, who shall be serving under articles in a certain town on a certain specified date, as the said trustee shall in his personal discretion deem to be most deserving of the same. The trustee dies after having made sale of the land and after having paid the debts and legacies. What disposition must be made of the balance of the proceeds? Give reasons.

A.—In *Burrough* v. *Philcox*, *5 My. & Cr. 72*, Lord Cottenham said: "When there appears a general intention in favour of a class, and a particular intention in favour of individuals of that class, and who are to be selected by another person, and the particular intention fails from that selection not being made, the Court will carry into effect the general intention in favour of the class." Equity follows the maxim that equality is equity, and divides the balance of the property equally among all the law students under articles in the town at the given date.

Snell, p. 109.

4. Q.—What is necessary in order to constitute a precatory trust, that is, what tests would you apply in order

to ascertain whether a certain form of words creates such
a trust ?

A.—A valid trust is created, (1) if the words are so used
that on the whole they ought to be construed as imperative
or certain, (2) if the subject-matter of the recommendation
or wish be certain, and (3) if the objects or persons intended
to have the benefit of the recommendation or wish be also
certain.

Snell, p. 101.

5. Q.—Define the equitable doctrine of election, and
illustrate your definition by an example.

A.—The doctrine of election originates in two inconsistent alternative donations or benefits, the one of which the
pretending donor has no power to make without at least
the assent of the donee of the other benefit. In this
duality of gifts, or pretended gifts, there is an intention,
which may be express, but which is more often implied,
that the one gift shall be a substitute for the other, that
the one gift shall take effect only if the donee thereof
permits the other gift to also take effect, substantially in
the manner and to the extent intended by the donor. The
permitting donee has the right to choose ; whence this head
of equity is commonly called *election*.

Example : A. by will devised to B. a farm which belonged
to C., and by the same will bequeathed to C. $15,000. C.
may elect against the will and keep his farm instead of
taking the $15,000, or he may elect to take the $15,000
under the will and give up his farm.

Snell, p. 241.

6. Q.—A. mortgages real estate in fee by a mortgage containing a power of sale. Default is made in payment and the

EQUITY. 75

property is sold under the power and a surplus is realized. In disposing of this surplus must the mortgagee treat it as real or personal estate? Would the question be in any way, and if so, in what way affected by the death of A.? Explain fully?

A.—If the estate had been sold by the mortgagee in the lifetime of the mortgagor, then the surplus money would have been personal estate of the mortgagor. But if the estate was unsold at the death of the mortgagor, the equity of redemption would descend to his heir, and he would be entitled to the surplus. Where the sale was before death, the surplus would go to the next of kin of the mortgagor.

Snell, p. 210.

But now, since the Devolution of Estates Act, the proceeds would go to the personal representatives of A. on his death.

7. Q.—State the general principles which, apart from statutory provisions or special provisions in the instrument creating the trusts, govern the courts of equity in determining the question whether or not a purchaser of land is bound to see to the application of the purchase money therefor, where he buys the same from a trustee thereof. What statutory provisions are there upon the subject?

A.—As to realty, where there is a trust or charge for the payment of debts and legacies generally, the purchaser is exonerated, but, where there is a trust for payment of certain debts or legacies only, the purchaser is not exonerated.

The provisions of the successive statutes bearing upon the matters have been as follows :—

Lord St. Leonard's Act, 22-23 Vict., c. 35, enacts that any person, paying purchase or mortgage money, shall be

exonerated unless the contrary shall be expressly declared
by the instrument creating the trust or security.

Lord Cranworth's Act, 23-24 Vict., c. 145, enacts that
the receipt in writing of any trustee, of any trust money
whatsoever, shall exonerate the purchaser. This applied
only to instruments coming into operation after August,
1860.

The Conveyancing Act, 44-45 Vict., c. 41, s. 36, enacts
that the receipt in writing of any trustee for any trust
moneys, securities, etc., whatever, under any trust or power,
shall be a sufficient discharge for the same, and shall effec-
tually exonerate the person paying, transferring, or delivering the same from seeing to the application or being
answerable for any loss or misapplication thereof. This
section of the Act applies to all trusts whensoever created
and whether before or after the Act.

The Settled Land Act, 1882, s. 40, contains a similar
power as regards funds arising under that Act, and this
Act also is retrospective.

   Snell, pp. 111 and 112.

8. Q.—Give a short statement of the law with respect to
setting aside contracts on account of the drunkenness of one
of the contracting parties.

A.—To set aside an act or contract on account of drunkenness, it is not sufficient that the party is under undue
excitement or lethargy from liquor. The excitement or
lethargy must arise to that degree in which the party is
utterly deprived for the time of the use of his reason and
understanding; for in such a case there can in no just
sense be said to be a serious and deliberate consent on his
part, and the court will grant relief. The court will also

grant relief if the party has, by some contrivance, been
induced to drink, or if some unfair advantage has been
taken in consequence of his intoxication. But, courts of
equity, as a matter of public policy, do not incline to lend
their assistance either to a person who has obtained a deed
or agreement from another in a state of intoxication, or to
the intoxicated party who wishes to get rid of his deed or
agreement merely on the ground of his intoxication at the
time.

     Snell, pp. 552 and 553.

9. Q.—A testator by his will leaves to A. power to
appoint certain of the testator's estate to such of the
children of the donee of the power as the donee shall
choose. A. for the purpose of acquiring the estate for his
own benefit makes an appointment to one of his children,
who is stricken down with a deadly disease, knowing that
the child must soon die, and that he will then himself in-
herit the property from the child. After the death of the
appointee the other children of A. claim an interest in the
property. What are their rights, if any?

A.—The other children have a right to the property. In
Hinchenbroke v. *Seymour*, *1 Bro. C. C. 394*, it was decided
that an appointment by a father to a sickly child for the
purpose of getting it back after the child's death is void,
and the father will not be allowed, on the child's death
under age, to derive any benefit from the appointment as
the personal representative of that child. The power must
be exercised *bona fide* for the end designed.

     Snell, p. 574.

10. Q.—State the difference between the rule at common
law and the rule in equity as to the right of a legatee to

bring action against an executor for the recovery of a legacy.

A.—A legatee may bring an action in equity against an executor for the recovery of a legacy, but no suit will lie at common law to recover legacies, unless the executor has assented thereto, or unless the action should be by the legatee of a debt against the executors and the debtor as co-defendants, where the executors refuse to sue the debtor. But in cases of specific legacies of goods, after the executor has assented thereto, the property vests immediately in the legatee, who may maintain an action at law for the recovery thereof.

Snell, p. 199.

11. Q.—A. sells to B. a dwelling house, but, unknown to either party at the time of making the deed, the house is swept away by a flood. Will a Court of Equity grant or refuse relief to the purchaser? Why? Under what head of equity-jurisprudence would this case come?

A.—This comes under the head of mistake of fact.

Under mistake or ignorance of a material fact the contract is voidable and relievable in equity. It matters not whether the mistake is that of one party only to the contract or is the mistake of both the parties. In *Bingham* v. *Bingham, 1 Ves. Sen. 126,* this case in question was decided and the purchaser was relieved upon the ground that both parties intended the purchase and sale of a subsisting thing, and implied its existence as the basis of their contract.

Snell, p. 527.

12. Q.—A surety is sued on a bond given to secure the faithful performance by a bank cashier of his duties, and the accounting by him for all moneys which he should

receive as such officer. His defence sets up that, at the
time he executed the bond, the cashier had embezzled the
funds of the bank, and that this was not disclosed to him,
though known to the officers of the bank when they applied
to him to go on the cashier's bond. Is this a good defence
or not ? Give reason for your answer.

A.—Story says : " If a party taking a guarantee from a
surety conceals from him facts *which go to increase his risk*,
and suffers him to enter into the contract under false im-
pressions as to the real state of facts, such concealment
will amount to fraud." In this case, therefore, there is a
sufficient degree of *suppressio veri* to annul the obligation
of the contract of suretyship, and it is a good defence to the
action.

Snell, p. 577.

13. Q.—A. is surety for the payment of a debt owing by
B. to C. C. also holds a mortgage on real estate of B.'s to
secure the same debt. C. at B.'s request releases the mortgage. How does this affect A.'s position ? Give reason
for your answer.

A.—If the creditor loses or allows securities to go back
into debtor's hands, this will discharge the surety to the
extent of such security. A. is discharged to the extent of
the mortgage because he is entitled on payment of the debt
to all the securities which the creditor has, or has ever
had, against the principal, and, since the creditor has
released the mortgage, the surety cannot be called upon to
pay that amount.

Snell, p. 589.

14. Q.—A. made an agreement in proper form to sell a
piece of land to B. but refused to make the conveyance.
What remedy had B. ?

A.—B. can enter an action for specific performance of the agreement; and if (as is usually the case) the damages at law, which must be calculated upon the general money value of the land, will not be a complete remedy to the purchaser, to whom the land may have a peculiar and special value, the Court will, on the ground simply of inadequacy of the damages, decree specific performance, but otherwise it will not do so.

    Snell, p. 631.

15. Q.—A. has a first mortgage on two pieces of land. B. has a second mortgage on one only of these pieces made by the same mortgagor. What course will a Court of Equity pursue upon foreclosure in order to protect both mortgagees as far as possible?

A.—The Court will direct A. (but always without prejudice to A.) to realise his debt out of that estate which is *not* in mortgage to B., so as to leave the one estate which is in mortgage to B. to satisfy B. so far as it goes.

    Lanoy v. *Duke of Athole, 2 A'k. 446.*
    Snell, p. 341.

16. Q.—If the creditor by binding contract, extends the time for payment of the debt by the debtor, without the consent of the surety; in what cases is the surety discharged and in what case is he not discharged? Give the reasons for your answer.

A.—If the remedies of the surety are thereby effected he will be discharged; but if the remedies of the surety are not thereby effected he will not be discharged. If the creditor giving time reserves his right against the surety, then the surety will not be discharged, for his remedy against the debtor still exists under the original contract.

The question to be considered in all these cases is whether the surety is in any way prejudiced as to his right against the original debtor.

Snell, p. 587 and 588.

17. Q.—A. and B. were in partnership as attorneys-at-law. A. bought real estate for the firm and gave a firm note without the knowledge of B. Is B. liable on the note or not and why?

A.—A. had no right to make such a note for it was not within the scope of the partnership business, and B. will not be liable on it.

18. Q.—A. who is the owner of a house and lot as trustee, in breach of his trust, sells it to B., who is cognizant of all the facts. With the proceeds A. buys a dwelling in his own name. Give all the remedies of the *cestui que trust*.

A.—The *cestui que trust* can follow the trust estate into the hands of the alienee if he be a volunteer, whether he had notice of the trust or not; and if the alienee be a purchaser of the estate even for valuable consideration, but with notice, the same rule applies.

Snell, p. 182 and 183.

If the trust estate has been tortiously disposed of by the trustee, the *cestui que trust* may attach and follow the property that has been substituted in the place of the trust estate, as long as the substituted property can be traced. Or he can have an action for damages against the trustee for breach of trust.

Snell, p. 185.

19. Q.—Define *equitable estoppel* and give an example.
Q.A.—6

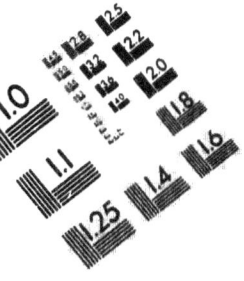

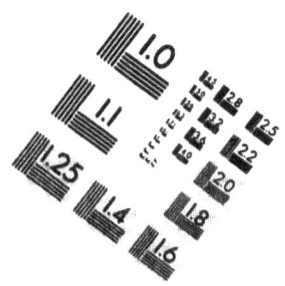

**IMAGE EVALUATION
TEST TARGET (MT-3)**

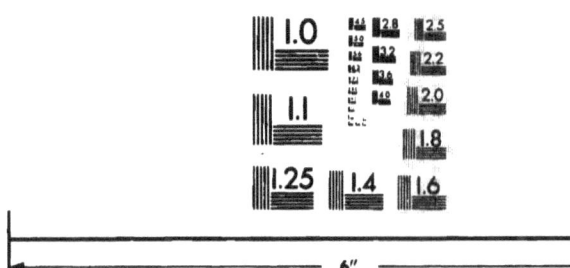

6"

Photographic
Sciences
Corporation

23 WEST MAIN STREET
WEBSTER, N.Y. 14580
(716) 872-4503

ό١

A.—*Equitable estoppels* or *estoppels in fact* apply to all cases where rights once valid are lost by delay. As, for example, where a party acquiesced in the violation of a covenant to a certain extent, this would afford sufficient objection to the granting of an interlocutory injunction against a greater violation of it.

Taylor, s. 1243.

20. Q.—What is a resulting trust ?   Give an example.

A.—Where property is conveyed on trusts, which do not exhaust the whole property, there will be a resulting trust of so much of the property, respecting which no trust is declared, in favor of the settlor.

As, for example, a devise in trust to pay debts is a devise for a particular purpose and nothing more, and the devisee will take no beneficial interest, and there will be a resulting trust of the balance after the debts are paid.

Snell, pp. 132 and 133.

21. Q.—Assets which have come to the hands of an administrator to be administered are without any fault on his part stolen from him. An action is brought by a creditor in which it is sought to make the administrator account for these assets. State the liability of the administrator.

A.—Trustees are bound to take in all cases the same care of the trust property as a man of ordinary caution would take of his own ; and if they have done so they will not be liable for any *accidental* loss ; as, for instance, by a robbery of the property while in their own possession, or by a robbery or loss whilst in the possession of others with whom it has necessarily, *i.e.*, in the ordinary course of business, been entrusted, or by a depreciation in the value of the securities upon which the trust funds are rightfully invested. But the Court, in determining the liability or non-liability of a trustee for any loss sustained by the trust estate, distinguishes between the *duties* imposed upon and *discretions* vested in him as such. And as regards his *duties*, the utmost diligence in observing the same (*i.e.*, *exacta diligentia*) is his only protection against liability for any loss ; and it is only as regards his *discretions*, or discretionary powers, that an amount of diligence equal to what he bestows on his own property will protect him from liability

Snell, pp. 156 and 157.

22. Q.—Distinguish between the different measures of relief afforded at law and in equity to one of several sureties who is compelled to pay the whole debt in a case where one of his co-sureties is insolvent.

A.—Formerly at common law he could only recover against the solvent sureties an *aliquot* part of the whole, regard being had to the original number of co-sureties ; but in equity the surety, who paid the entire debt could compel the solvent sureties to contribute *pro rata* towards payment of the entire debt. But now this difference is abolished.

Snell, p. 585.

23. Q.—On the administration of an estate a certain fund has been handed over by the executor to the residuary legatee. At the time of handing over this fund the executor had sufficient funds in hand to satisfy all general legacies, which funds he afterwards wasted. An unpaid general legatee seeks by action to compel the residuary legatee to refund the moneys, which have been paid to him in order that the same may be applied in payment of gen-

eral legacies. What are the respective rights of the parties to the action ?

A.—The unpaid general legatee has no right against the residuary legatee, and can only recover against the trustee for a breach of trust.

> Taylor, s. 428.

24. Q.– When will an action *quia timet* lie ?

A.—Even since the Judicature Act, an action in the nature of a bill *quia timet* may still be brought; but no such action will lie unless the plaintiff is able to prove imminent danger of a substantial kind, or that the apprehended injury, if it does come, will be irreparable.

> Snell, p. 723.

25. Q.—What jurisdiction have the Courts of this Province with regard to alimony, and whence is that jurisdiction derived ?

A.—By the Judicature Act, R. S. O. c. 44 s. 29 :—" The High Court shall have jurisdiction to grant alimony to any wife who would be entitled to alimony by the law of England, or to any wife who would be entitled by the law of England to a divorce and to alimony as incident thereto, and to any wife whose husband lives separate from her without any sufficient cause and under circumstances which would entitle her, by the law of England, to a decree for restitution of conjugal rights : and alimony where granted shall continue until the further order of the Court."

> Taylor, ss. 1191-1197.

26. Q.—Illustrate by two examples the difference between the doctrine of law and of equity, giving cases where

relief would be afforded to a suitor in equity which would be refused to him at common law, and give one example of a case where relief would be afforded to a suitor at common law which would be refused to him in equity?

A.—The distinction between law and equity is not so much of substance as of form—a distinction not of principle but of history. Equity is that portion of natural justice which is of a nature to be judicially enforced, but which the Courts of Common Law omitted to enforce.

Snell, p. 2.

Examples: An outstanding dry legal term prior in date to the plaintiff's title to an estate, although it was a merely technical objection, yet it would at law have prevented the plaint'ff from recovering in ejectment; here the Court of Equity would interpose and put the ter. out of the plaintiff's way, and would permit the plaintiff by an ejectment bill to get actual possession.

Snell, p. 10.

Specific performance could only be got in equity.

Snell, p. 627.

Where the remed" was complete at law equity would not interfere, as, in a breach of a contract for the sale of ordinary chattels, the Common Law Courts would grant damages and equity would not interfere.

27. Q.—Give an example of a case where a Court of Equity could decree specific performance of part of an agreement and not of another part?

A.—It occasionally happens that an agreement comprising two or more matters, some of which if they stood alone would be specifically enforceable, while others of them (either because of illegality or for some other reason) are not specifically enforceable. Example: A building agreement containing a provision for granting leases piecemeal to the builder or his assigns upon completion of the buildings on the several plots. If the conditions as to building on any plot have been fulfilled, the Court will enforce the agreement to grant a lease of that plot, even though the buildings have not been erected on the other plots, and the Court could not enforce specifically the agreement to build.

Snell, p. 680.

28. Q.—Illustrate by example the doctrine of *cy-pres*.

A.—A bequest of the residue of the testator's estate to a company to apply the interest of a moiety "unto the redemption of British slaves in Turkey and Barbary," one-fourth to charity schools in London, and one-fourth to the poor and destitute freemen of the company. There being no British slaves in Turkey and Barbary, the Court decreed a new scheme to be framed *cy-pres*, and approved of a scheme which gave the moiety thus undisposed of to the donees of the other fourth parts.

Snell, p. 120.

29. Q.—A. conveys certain lands unto and to the use of B. in trust to support C. during his life, and then to hold to the use of A. The grantor then dies intestate and without heirs, and subsequently C. dies. The Crown claims the property by virtue of its prerogative right to escheated lands. Who is entitled to the property and why?

A.—B. is entitled to the property. For as to realty the trustee used to take beneficially, because, if the trustee was seized in fee, there would be no *escheat*. So also where a mortgage in fee was made, and the mortgagor died intestate and without heirs, the equity of redemption did not *escheat*, but belonged to the mortgagee, subject to the mortgagor's debts and wife's dower.

But, in England, under the Intestates Estates Act, 1884, the real estate would in all cases *escheat* to the Crown or Lord. And apparently the Act in question extends also to money directed to be converted into real estate, for such money as being "equitable realty" would fall within the 4th section of the Act.

Snell, pp. 134 and 135.

30. Q.—Where an award has been duly made directing one of the parties to allow to another of the parties a right of way over a certain lane, and he refuses to do so, what equitable relief, if any, may be obtained by the person in whose favor the award is made?

A.—He can apply to the Court for an injunction restraining the other party from preventing him using the right of way, and the Court will grant it.

31. Q.—Define *executed* and *executory* trusts, and state the distinction between the *rules of construction* applicable to *executed trusts* and *executory trusts* respectively, and illustrate by example of each.

A.—A trust is said to be *executed* when no act is necessary to be done to constitute it, the trust being finally declared by the instrument creating it. A trust is said to be *executory* when there is a mere direction to convey upon certain trusts, and the instrument containing the direction to convey does not of itself, *proprio vigore*, constitute the trust or effect the conveyance which it directs.

Lord St. Leonards says: "A Court of Equity, in considering an *executory* trust as distinguished from an *executed* trust, distinguishes the two in this manner : Has the testator been what is called, and very properly called, his own conveyancer ? Or has he, on the other hand, left it to the Court to make out from *general expressions* what his intention is ? If he has so defined that intention that you have nothing to do but to take the limitations he has given to you, and to convert them into legal estates, then the trust is *executed*, but otherwise it is *executory*."

As to construction of executed trusts. " Equity follows the law." If an estate is vested in trustees and their heirs in trust for A. for life, without impeachment of waste, with the remainder to trustees to preserve contingent remainders, with remainder in trust for the heirs of the body of A., the trust being an *executed* trust, A., according to the rule in *Shelley's case*, which is a rule of law, will be held to take an estate tail. There is no exception to this rule.

As to construction of executory trusts. " Equity may or may not follow the law." *Executory* trusts are found in two documents only, *i.e.*, marriage articles and wills. In marriage articles *intention* is always implied. Their object is, of course, to make a provision for the issue of the marriage. In wills intention is required to be expressed. In marriage articles the Court will decree a strict settlement in conformity with presumed intention. By the rule in *Shelley's case*, both or either husband or wife might take an estate tail and be able to defeat the issue, but the Court will decree a strict settlement and give husband and wife estate for life, only, with remainder to issue in tail as purchasers. In wills the Court will construe strictly in the absence of expressed intention to the contrary, and will construe according to the contrary intention if that be expressed.

Snell, pp. 55 *et seq.*

82. Q.—A. sells a farm to B. by a parol agreement, which provides that B. shall not be entitled to possession until the expiry of the term of the present tenant, which will be three months hence. B., however, forthwith takes forcible possession and proceeds to make improvements on the farm. A. subsequently refuses to complete the contract, whereupon B. brings action for specific performance relying upon the doctrine of part performance. Who should succeed in the action and why?

A.—B. took forcible possession, and, therefore, not under the verbal contract. He was a trespasser and wrong-doer, and this could not be called a part performance of the verbal agreement, and would not take the case out of the Statute of Frauds. Hence, specific performance would not be granted. If he had been *let into* possession, or if possession had been *delivered* to him, it would then have been a part performance sufficient to take the case out of the Statute, and he would succeed in his action.

Snell, p. 639.

83. Q.—Give an example of a valid restraint on marriage annexed to a legacy, and another of an attempted restraint which is invalid as being *in terrorem.*

A.—A legacy given to a daughter to be paid to her at twenty-one if she does not marry until that period would be valid ; but a legacy to a daughter, on condition that she should not marry a man who was not seized of an estate in fee simple of the clear yearly value of £500, would not be valid, on the ground that the condition is *in terrorem* only and does not impose a forfeiture.

Taylor, ss. 195 and 196.

34. Q.--In case of an election, what is the effect of the donee electing against the instruments ?   Illustrate by an example.

A.—*Compensation* and not *forfeiture* is the rule upon an election by the donee against the instrument.

Example : A. gives B. by will a legacy of £30,000, and gives C. by the same will an estate belonging to B. valued at £20,000.   B. elects against the will and keeps his estate, and will get £10,000 of the legacy; and C. will get the remaining £20,000 of the legacy.

Snell, p. 244.

35. Q.—Is a voluntary verbal declaration of trust of certain property by the owner thereof ever effectual, and if so, under what circumstances ?   Is the question affected by statute, and if so, how ?

A.—A voluntary verbal declaration of trust is effectual if of pure personal estate, *i.e., chattels personal,* for personal estate is not within the Act, except so far as the assignment or transfer of an already created and subsisting trust is concerned.   But all realty (including chattels real) is included within the Statute of Frauds and a declaration of trust concerning it must be in writing.

Snell, pp. 53 and 54.

36. Q.—Where some right, title or interest in land is in question in an action, what step can the plaintiff take in order to prevent the land from falling into the hands of an innocent purchaser for value, without notice of the plaintiff's right ?

A.—The·plaintiff may register a *lis pendens.*

87. Q.—What is the rule in equity as to the right of a solicitor to purchase property from his client during the continuance of the relationship?

A.—A gift from a client to a solicitor pending that relationship cannot stand, but a purchase by a solicitor from a client, if there is perfect *bona fides*, is good.

Snell, p. 563.

But now a solicitor can take a gift by will from his client.

88. Q.—A. and B. enter into a valid contract for the formation of a partnership at will. A. subsequently refuses to enter into the partnership. Will a Court of Equity afford B. any, and if so, what relief? Explain clearly.

A.—Equity will decree specific performance of an agreement to enter into a partnership for a *fixed and definite period of time*, if there have been acts of part performance; but it will not do so when no term has been fixed, for such a decree would be useless when either of the parties might dissolve the partnership immediately afterwards.

Snell, p. 592.

89. Q.—Mention some of the cases in which the Court will order an account between partners without any view to an ultimate dissolution of the partnership?

A.—Where no dissolution is intended or prayed the general rule is that, where a partner has been wrongfully excluded or the conduct of the other partner has been such as would entitle the complaining partner to a dissolution as against him, a general account, at any rate up to the time of filing the bill, will be decreed: but that in no case will a continuous account be decreed as that would be, in part at least, a carrying on of the business by the Court.

Snell, p. 600.

40. Q.—Illustrate by an example the maxim that " a trust shall not fail for want of a trustee " ?

A.—Where property has been bequeathed in trust without the appointment of a trustee, if it is personal estate, the personal representative is deemed the trustee; if it is real estate, the heir. If the trustee dies the Court will appoint a new one ; and when the trustee is not named, and there is no one who can properly execute the trust, the Court will assume the office first and then appoint a trustee afterwards.

Snell, p. 152.

41. Q.—State under what circumstances a Court of Equity will decree a dissolution of partnership at the instance of one of the partners.

A.—The Court will decree a dissolution of partnership, at the instance of one of the partners, where induced by fraud, gross misconduct and breach of trust, continual breaches of contract, wilful and permanent neglect of business, disagreement or incompatibility of temper when it is such as to make it impossible to carry on the business, and insanity of partner whose skill is indispensable.

Snell, pp. 597 et seq.

42. Q.—A. enters into a parol agreement with B. for the purchase of Black acre at $100,000. B. pays $5,000, when A. refuses to carry out the contract. Can B. compel him ? What, if any, difference would there be in B.'s rights if he had gone into possession of the property ?

A.—Mere payment of part of the purchase money is not sufficient part performance of the parol agreement to take it out of the operation of the Statute of Frauds. If he had

gone into possession or commenced improvements under
the agreement he could then have compelled A. to complete the agreement.

(Compare Question No. 32, *ante*.)

Snell, pp. 639 and 640.

43. Q.—An executor at the time of entering on his duties
as such is in possession of abundant assets to pay all liabilities, but through no fault of his own, loses so large a portion of the assets by the failure of an apparently solvent
bank that he is unable to pay the creditors. One of these
sues him for the debt due from the estate, and the executor
consults you as to his position. How would you advise
him ?

A.—If the executor has not been at fault in any way of
course he would not be liable. He would be liable for wilful default or neglect.

Snell, pp. 167-172 and 386.

44. Q.—A. by his will charges his real estate with the
payment of his debts generally ; he then devises his real
estate to trustees in trust for various other persons. Have
the trustees any and what powers as to selling or to mort-
gaging the real estate ?

A.—Subject to the provisions of the Devolution of
Estates Act, the personal estate is primarily liable for the
payment of debts, and when it is attempted to exonerate
the personal estate at the expense of the real estate, very
clear language is required. To do this he must show an
intention not only to charge his real estate with his debts,
but also to exonerate his personal estate. Therefore neither a general charge of debts upon the real estate, nor an

express trust created by the testator for the payment of
debts out of the real estate, will be sufficient. In this case
in question the real estate would only be subject to sale or
mortgage in the event of the personal estate failing to
satisfy all the debts.

Snell, p. 322.

45. Q.—A. and B., husband and wife, are living apart.
A suit for alimony is brought. What will be necessary for
the wife to show in order to succeed ? At what stage of
the proceedings will the Court grant interim alimony ?

A.—As to what is necessary for the wife to show in
order to succeed, see Question No. 25 *ante*, and as to
interim alimony see

C. R. P., No. 530.

46. Q.—State under what circumstances the giving of
time by a creditor to the principal debtor will discharge
the surety, and when not.

A.—If the creditor gives time in a binding manner to the
debtor without the consent of the surety, and thereby
effects the remedies of the surety, the surety will be discharged ; but if his remedies are not effected, or if the
creditor giving time reserves his right against the surety,
then the surety will not be discharged. (Compare Question
No. 16, *ante*.)

Snell, p. 587.

47. Q.—What is necessary in a voluntary settlement to
support the same as against creditors ?

A.—If the settlor is solvent and the settlement is not
made to defeat creditors it is good ; and it is only where

ryment of
ı this case
to sale or
failing to

ing apart.
cessary for
ıt stage of
mony?
;o show in
and as to

e giving of
l discharge

ınner to the
nd thereby
will be dis-
:l, or if the
the surety,
ıre Question

ıttlement to

ment is not
ı only where

creditors are delayed seriously by the settlement in getting paid their debts that the settlement is made void.

Snell, pp. 75 *et seq.*

48. Q.—A party claiming to have some right, title or interest in certain lots in Toronto comes to you to consult as to the proper steps to be taken, in order to prevent the lots falling into possession of a third party for value without notice of your client's supposed rights. What course would you advise him to pursue?

A.—He should be advised to enter an action claiming whatever title or interest or lien he is entitled to, and then register a *lis pendens* against the property.

49. Q.—An infant in the course of a contract by which he sells and conveys lands represents himself to be of age. He afterwards attempts to repudiate the contract by refusing to give possession, setting up his infancy as the ground of refusal. How should he succeed? Explain fully.

A.—Infants are generally favored by law as well as by equity in all things which are for their benefit, and are saved from being prejudiced by anything which is to their disadvantage. But this rule is designed as a shield for their own protection, and not as a means to perpetrate a fraud or injustice on others. Hence in this case in question the infant would not be allowed to repudiate the contract unless he gives up all the benefits he has acquired thereunder.

Snell, p. 554.

50. Q.—A. by his will leaves an annuity to be secured in certain public stock, and appoints C. as a residuary legatee.

Stock is purchased sufficient for the purpose, but by Act of Parliament is afterwards reduced. What are the rights of the annuitant and the residuary legatee as between each other ?

A.—Equity will decree the loss to be made up from the residuary legatee in favor of the annuitant.

     Taylor, s. 73.

51. Q.—A trustee for the sale of lands purchases them himself. The *cestui que trust* on discovering the fact enters an action to have the sale set aside. The trustee puts in a defence that he paid full value. Who should succeed ? Explain the general law.

A.—Generally the trustee cannot purchase. But

(1) If the trustee will give more than any one else, *i.e.*, a "fancy price," or

(2) If the offer to sell proceeds from the *cestui qui trustent* and the trustee pays ordinary value, keeping the *cestui qui trustent* at arm's length, or

(3) If the sale is by auction, and the trustee has leave of the Court to bid,

Then the purchase by the trustee will in general hold good.

Or if by lapse of time or by subsequent events it becomes impossible of recision, then it will continue.

In the case in question the trustee's defence would not be sufficient, for he should show that he gave a "fancy price."

     Snell, p. 161.

52. Q.—What circumstances will it be necessary for you to prove in order to successfully impeach a voluntary

it by Act of
he rights of
tween each

p from the

hases them
e fact enters
ee puts in a
ld succeed ?

But
ne else, *i.e.*,

i qui *trustent*
the *cestui q.ii*

has leave of

general hold

ts it becomes

ce would not
ve a "fancy

ssary for you
a voluntary

settlement under 13 Elizabeth, chap. 5 ? Is there any Provincial legislation affecting the same ?

A.—The settlor must have been at the time not necessarily insolvent, but so largely indebted as to induce the Court to believe that the intention of the settlement, taking the whole transaction together, was to defraud the persons who at the time of making the settlement were creditors of the settlor. The settlor must have been embarrassed at the date of the settlement, or must have become immediately so in consequence thereof. This is effected by the Act Respecting Voluntary and Fraudulent Conveyances, which says: " Where there is any fraud a voluntary conveyance, or even a conveyance with consideration in the absence of *bona fides*, is void against creditors," etc. There must be *bona fides* without notice of fraud. This Act applies since March, 1872.

Snell, p. 78.
R. S. O., c. 96.

53. Q.—What is meant by an illusory appointment ? Illustrate.

A.—When a person, having power of appointment to members of a class, although with full discretion as to the amount of their respective shares, exercised that power by appointing to one or more a merely nominal share, such an appointment though valid at law was set aside as illusory, not being exercised *bona fide* for the end designed by the donor. Wm. IV. c. 46 abolished this doctrine in 1830, and now by Powers' Amendment Act, 1874 (hereafter), the appointor need not now appoint any share, unless the power expressly directs that no object of the power is to receive less than a specified amount.

Snell, p. 575.
Q. A.—7

54. Q.—A person believing himself to be the owner of a lot of land proceeds to erect buildings, with the knowledge of the real owner, who says nothing to him of his mistake. What remedy, if any, has he on ejectment proceedings being brought against him ?

A.—In such cases, the person who has expended money will, in equity, be indemnified for his expenditure on eviction by the real owner, for it would be inequitable for him to profit by his own fraud.

Snell, p. 682.

55. Q.—A. dies intestate. Administration is taken out in a foreign country, and also in this country. The foreign administrator collects the assets in the foreign country and remits them here. Which administrator *is entitled* to those assets so remitted ?

A.—The foreign administrator *will be entitled* to the assets so remitted.

Taylor, s. 423.

56. Q.—A. sold B. certain land at the ordinary price for farm land. B. knew when buying that the land was of far greater value than A. supposed it to be, on account of the existence of a fine stone quarry of which A. was ignorant. Can A. repudiate the sale ?

A.—The principles on which mistake of fact are relievable are :—(1) The fact must be material. (2) The fact must be such as the party could not get knowledge of by diligent enquiry. (3) The party having knowledge must have been under an obligation to discover the fact. (4) Where the means of information are equally open to both, and there is no confidence reposed, no relief will be granted.

In this case in question B. was under no obligation to make the fact of the quarry known, and no confidence was reposed, but each dealt at arm's length. Therefore A. cannot repudiate the sale.

Snell, pp. 527 and 528.

57. Q.—Under what circumstances will a Court of Equity decree specific performance of an agreement to enter into a partnership?

A.—Equity will enforce specific performance of an agreement to enter into a partnership for *a definite time* where there have been *acts of part of performance.*

Snell, p. 592 and 593.

58. Q.—Distinguish between the doctrines of *tacking* and *consolidation* of mortgages. Is there any Provincial legislation affecting the same? If so what?

A.—The doctrine of *consolidation* depends upon a principle altogether different from that upon which *tacking* depends. Because in *tacking*, the right is to throw together several debts lent on the *same* estate, and to do so under the priority and protection afforded by the legal estate; but in *consolidation*, the right is to throw together on one estate several debts lent on *different* estates, and to do so *without reference to any priority or protection afforded by the legal estate*, but solely upon the equitable maxim that he who seeks equity must do equity.

Snell, pp. 883 and 884.

As to the legislation upon this subject, see Conveyancing Act, 1881 (44 and 45 Vict. c. 41), s. 17.

R. S. O., c. 114, s. 88.

59. Q.—A. by his will bequeaths $10,000 to trustees for such charitable or public purposes as the trustees in their discretion shall think fit. Is the bequest good? Explain.

A.—The legacy cannot be supported and the property will in general devolve on the next of kin of the testator. It is void because it is not exclusively charitable, and it is also too general and indefinite for the Court to execute. If the gift were for charity alone equity would execute it at all events.

Snell, p. 118.

60. Q.—Are there any statutory provisions affecting the right of a mortgagee whose interest is in arrears pursuing all his remedies at once? If so, what?

A.—When demand of payment is made, or notice of intention to exercise power of sale is given, no further proceedings can be taken until expiration of time named in the notice or demand, unless by order of a judge.

R. S. O., c. 102, s. 30.

61. Q.—In what cases will a Court of Equity in no event interfere to mitigate a penalty or forfeit when incurred?

A.—The High Court is enabled to give relief upon equitable terms against every *forfeiture* for a breach of any covenant whatsoever contained in a lease or under lease or farm grant, other than and except only the following covenants and conditions, viz.:

(1) Condition of forfeiture upon bankruptcy or execution.

(2) Covenant not to assign or underlet.

(3) Covenant in a mining lease for permitting inspection, etc., by lessor.

Snell, p. 421.

When any penalty or forfeiture is imposed by Statute a Court of Equity will not interfere.

Taylor, s. 1110.

62. Q.—What was, and what is now the law with regard to the employment of puffers at auction sales of lands?

A.—If puffers were employed at a sale of land to deceive other bidders, and they were in fact misled, the sale would be held void as against public policy. But now by Statute the vendors may reserve the right to bid in regard to real or personal property, and there would be no fraud.

R. S. O., c. 100, ss. 23 and 24.

[N.B.—From this collection on equity there have been excluded twenty-three questions which were repeated. F. L. W.]

CHAPTER IV.

MERCANTILE LAW.

STATUTES AND PRACTICE.

1. Q.—A., B. and C. are in partnership carrying on mercantile business in the name of A. & Co. C. goes out of the firm, which is still carried on under the same name. What must C. do to escape liability for debts of the firm after he leaves?

A.—C. must advertise his removal from the firm if he wishes to escape liability after leaving. An advertisement in the *Gazette* is notice to all persons, but it is usual to send a special notice to the customers.

Smith, pp. 45 and 46.

2. Q.—To what extent is an infant partner bound by the liabilities of his firm?

A.—Infants are not liable except for necessaries. An infant entering into a contract of partnership incurs no liability for the debts of the firm. But if he does not within a reasonable time after coming of age repudiate the contract, he will be held liable as a partner for acts done after that event. If he has obtained advantage under a contract, *e.g.*, received goods, and cannot place the person contracting with him in the same position as before the contract, he cannot recover money which he has paid, and he cannot share in the profits without contributing to the losses.

Smith, p. 5.

3. Q.—Define the rights of an endorsee or a bill of lading ?

A.—The negotiation of a bill of lading transfers the property in the goods which the consignee had with all his rights of action, and it may defeat the consignor's right to *stoppage in transitu.*

Smith, pp. 345 *et seq.*

4. Q.—A. owes B. a debt, which B. assigns to C. A. without knowledge of the assignment buys an overdue promissory note made by B. for half the amount of his debt to B. Define the rights and liabilities of A., B. and C. respectively in regard to the premises ?

A.—C. should have given A. notice of the assignment, and since he did not do so, A. will be entitled to a set-off against C. for the amount of the note made by B. Where A. is allowed a set-off for the amount of the note, then C. will be entitled to the note which he can enforce against B.

5. Q.—Define *general average.*

A.—*General average* is the contribution made by the parties to an adventure towards a loss, consisting in the sacrifices made or expenses incurred by some of them, for the common benefit of the ship and cargo.

Wharton's Law Lexicon, p. 326.

6. Q.—In what way can the amount secured on a life insurance policy be kept clear of the demands of creditors ?

A.—The insured may declare the policy for the benefit of his wife, or his wife and children, or any of them, and when this is so stated in the policy, or endorsed on it, or stated by a written declaration referring to the policy, such policy shall ensure to the benefit of such persons, and so long as any object remains it shall not be subject to the control of the husband or his creditors. But if premiums are paid in fraud of the creditors, they may recover so much as has been fraudulently paid.

R. S. O., c. 186, s. 5.

7. Q.—What provisions are made by statute to prevent unfairness in the conditions on a policy of fire insurance ?

A.—If the company desires to vary the statutory conditions, or to omit any of them, or to add new conditions, there shall be added on the instrument of contract containing the printed statutory conditions words to the following effect, printed in conspicuous type, and in ink of a different colour :—" Variations in conditions, etc., etc." And no such variation shall be valid unless so set forth, and unless it be just and reasonable.

R. S. O., c. 167, ss. 115 and 116.

8. Q.—In how far is a person against whom a defendant in an action claims to be indemnified from the result of the action, bound by the result, where he has been served with notice under the Judicature Act as a third party to the action, and fails to appear ?

A.—He shall be deemed to admit the validity of the judgment obtained against such defendant, whether obtained by consent or otherwise, provided always that a person so in default may apply for leave to appeal.

C. R. P., No. 331.

9. Q.—When must a demurrer be set down for argument ?

A.—Demurrers must be set down for argument six clear days before hearing, and a copy of the demurrer book or special case must be left with the Clerk of Records and Writs two days before hearing.

C. R. P., No. 540.

10. Q.—What peculiar requirements and provisions have been attached to promissory notes given for the purchase of patent rights?

A.—The words "given for a patent right" must be written or printed across the face thereof. The transferee of any such instrument shall take the same subject to any defence or set-off, in respect of the whole or any part thereof, which would have existed between the original parties. The penalty for uttering such an instrument not so marked is a misdemeanour, punishable by imprisonment for any term not exceeding one year, or by fine not exceeding two hundred dollars.

R. S. C., c. 123, ss. 12, 13 and 14.

11. Q.—Can community of profit be depended on as a criterion for ascertaining whether two individuals are partners, and why?

A.—It is not by itself a presumption of the existence of a partnership, but it is strong evidence of such existence. A servant might be paid by a given portion of the profits, and yet might not be a partner. The criterion is whether or not they can act as agents of one another within the scope of the business.

Smith, p. 10.

12. Q.—State shortly the proper method of giving notice of the dissolution of a partnership firm?

A.—Notice in the *Gazette* is notice to all parties. It is also usual to advertise in other papers, and to send notices to the regular customers of the firm.

Smith, pp. 45 and 46.

13. Q.—Under what circumstances, if any, will an agent contracting for a known principal incur personal liability?

A.—He incurs no liability unless he expressly binds himself, or unless he contracts under seal, or for a foreign principal.

Smith, p. 173.

14. Q.—Trace the history of negotiability of bills of lading?

A.—A bill of lading is not negotiable in the sense in in which a bill of exchange or promissory note is; property does not pass by mere delivery to a *bona fide* holder for valuable consideration; it is negotiable only as a symbol of the goods. Its indorsement, too, formerly transferred no more than the property in the goods—it did not transfer the contract between the original parties to it. But by statute the indorsee was given all the rights and liabilities as if the bill had been made with himself.

Smith, pp. 346 and 347.

15. Q.—What is the rule as to the passing of property in goods sold where the date of payment of price or delivery of goods or both are postponed?

A.—The passing of the property depends on the intention of the vendor and vendee. The vendor may retain possession and exercise his right to lien, or he may give this up by selling on credit and delivering over goods.

16. Q.—A. owes B. $100, and B. agrees to accept $50 in full. The $50 is paid. Is the agreement to accept in full binding ?

A.—Yes. The agreement is binding by
R. S. O., c. 44, s. 58, s-s. 7.

17. Q.—In what cases may service of a writ of summons, or notice of such writ, be allowed out of Ontario ?

A.—Service is allowed out of Ontario when the action is for (a) land in Ontario, or (b) anything affecting land in Ontario, or (c) when the action is against a person domiciled or ordinarily resident within Ontario, or (d) for administration of personal estate of a person who died in Ontario, or (e) where the action is on a contract which ought to be performed within Ontario wherever made, or (f) for an injunction against anything in Ontario, or (g) when any person outside is a proper party to an action brought properly against others within the jurisdiction.

C. R. P., No. 271.

18. Q.—Where pleadings are amended without leave, and such amendments are improper, how may they be objected to by the opposite side ?

A.—The opposite party can, within eight days after the amended pleading is delivered to him, apply to the Court or a Judge to disallow the amendment.

C. R. P., No. 426.

19. Q.—Indicate changes made in the law affecting the priorities of judgment creditors having executions in the hands of a sheriff.

A.—There are no priorities now. The sheriff levies and enters notice thereof, and then distributes ratably to all who have writs, or certificates given under the Act, in the sheriff's hands at the time of the levy, or within one month after the entry of the notice, subject, however, to the provisions as to the retention of dividends in the case of contested claims, and to the payment of the costs of the creditor under whose writ the amount was made.

R. S. O., c. 65, ss. 3 and 4.

20. Q.—What difference, in consequence of a special agent exceeding his authority, from that of a general agent so doing?

A.—The authority of an agent to perform all things usual, *i.e.*, a *general agent*, cannot be limited by any private order or direction not known to the party dealing with him. The Rule is directly the reverse concerning a *particular agent*. It is the duty of a party dealing with such a one to ascertain the extent of his authority, otherwise he must abide the consequences.

Smith, pp. 139 and 140.

21. Q.—A. wishes to sue B. upon a cheque for $90 and an open account of $106. In what Court must he sue? What authority for your statement?

A.—He must sue in the County Court. If the open account had been for $100 or less, then his action would have been within the jurisdiction of the Division Court.

R. S. O., c. 51, s. 70.

22. Q.—What are the rules as to the admissibility of defences in suits upon judgments obtained in the Province of Quebec?

A.—In suits brought upon judgments obtained in Quebec, if the process was served personally there is no defence, but if not served personally, any defence that might have been set up to the original suit may be made to the suit on the judgment in Ontario.

R. S. O., c. 44, ss. 81 and 82.

23. Q.—What are the statutory provisions as to the right to claim interest on open accounts ?

A.—Interest may be allowed from the time when a demand of payment is made in writing informing the debtor that interest will be claimed from the date of the demand.

R. S. O., c. 44, s. 90.

24. Q.—In what cases is corroboration of plaintiff's testimony required to obtain a verdict ?

A.—The plaintiff's testimony must be corroborated in actions for breach of promise, and in actions against a lunatic or the personal representatives of a deceased person.

R. S. O., c. 61, ss. 6, 10 and 11.

25. Q.—When can you obtain a *transcript* of a Division Court judgment to a County Court ?

A.—In case an execution is returned *nulla bona*, and the sum remaining unsatisfied on the judgment under which the execution issued amounts to the sum of $40, the plaintiff or defendant may obtain a *transcript* of the judgment from the clerk, under his hand and sealed with the seal of the Court, and, upon filing the *transcript* in the office of the County Court Clerk, the same shall become a judgment of the County Court.

R. S. O., c. 51, ss. 223 and 224.

26. Q.—Explain fully what liability is incurred by an acceptance *for honor*.

A.—An acceptor *for honor* engages that he will, on due presentment, pay the bill according to the tenor of his acceptance, if it is not paid by the drawee, provided it has been duly presented for payment and protested for non-payment, and that he receives notice of these facts. He is liable to the holder, and to all parties to the bill subsequent to the party for whose honor he has accepted. The engagement of an acceptor *for honor* differs from that of an ordinary acceptor ; it is conditional on due presentment, and notice of dishonor, and protest of the bill. It is equivalent to saying to the holder: "Keep the bill, do not return it ; and when the time arrives at which it ought to be paid, if it be not paid by the party on whom it is drawn, come to me, and you shall have the money." In order, therefore, to complete the liability of the acceptor *for honor*, the bill must be presented for payment when it falls due, notwithstanding the former refusal of the drawee, who may possibly in the meantime have received assets. This presentment must be followed by protest of the bill for non-payment before it is presented for payment to the acceptor *for honor*. When it is dishonored by the acceptor *for honor* it must be protested for non-payment.

Smith, p. 259.

27. Q.—A. is a tradesman and wishes to purchase goods from B. B. requires security. A. offers the bond of C. and D. A bond is prepared for execution by C. and D. Both are notified, and C. executes, but D. does not. In case of loss how far is C. liable, and why ?

A.—If there are two or more sureties, the release of one discharges the others in all cases where the obligation of the co-sureties is *joint* or *joint and several*, for there the joint suretyship of the others is part of the consideration

, on due
r of his
ed it has
for non-
. He is
ll subse-
ed. The
n that of
entment,
t is equi-
l, do not
ought to
is drawn,
In order,
eptor *for*
en it falls
awee, who
its. This
e bill for
it to the
acceptor

ase goods
ond of C.
C. and D.
not. In

ase of one
igation of
there the
sideration

for the contract of each. Where the sureties are bound
severally only, the suretyship of the one is no part of the
contract of the others, except in cases where, and to the
extent to which, the right of contribution is thereby lost
to the others.

In this case in question C. is not liable because he only
agreed to be surety along with D. and, since D. did not
execute the bond, C. is discharged.

Smith, p. 587.

28. Q.—How far is a solicitor by his duty required to
consult counsel? What security does he gain by so doing?

A.—He is not required to do so, but he relieves himself
of liability by so doing.

29. Q.—How far can one partner bind by deed the firm
of which he is a member?

A.—A partner may bind the firm by simple contract,
but he cannot bind them by deed unless he has express
authority by deed for that purpose.

Smith, p. 33.

30. Q.—A. applies to an insurance company to insure
the life of B. The company apply to B. for information
as to his physical condition, which B. falsely misstates.
How far is A. liable for these misrepresentations? Why?

A.—B. is not the agent of A. and, therefore, A. is not
bound by B.'s statements, and, in the absence of any condition to that effect, or fraud on his own part, will not
suffer should they be false.

Everett v. *Desborough, 5 Bing. 503.*
Wheelton v. *Hardisty, 8 E. & B. 232.*
Smith, pp. 499 and 500.

31. Q.—A. is surety for B.'s debt to C. The latter, without communicating with A., takes a chattel mortgage to further secure the indebtedness of B. How is A.'s position affected ?

A.—A. is in no way prejudiced by this and is still liable as surety ; but in case he is compelled to pay he will then be entitled to all the securities C. has or has ever had, including the chattel mortgage.

32. Q.—A. buys in Montreal fifty cases of broadcloths from B. worth $500 on terms of two months' credit. The goods are in store at C.'s warehouse in Toronto. B. gives A. an order on C. for the purchased goods. A. presents the order in Toronto to C. The latter finds an entry of only forty cases and says he will accept for that amount, which he does. A. thereupon writes to B. informing him of what has taken place. B. then writes back saying he will not carry out the contract and notifies C. not to hand over the goods he has. What are the rights and liabilities of the parties ?

A.—A. accepted the forty cases and the property in them passed.

A. is entitled to recover the forty cases and enter an action against B. for the non-delivery of the balance.

33. Q.—A. is in debt to B. on an account which B. claims to amount to $500. A. claims that there is only $450 due. He makes a tender to B. for $450 in gold and says " Here are $450. I want your receipt in full." B. refuses to accept it, claiming that there is more due. On a subsequent taking of accounts it was found that the amount due was $450. Was the tender good ? Why ?

A.—The tender is not good. No tender is good if accompanied by a condition, as the demand for a document to be cancelled, or for a receipt in full.

Smith, p. 667.

34. Q.—A., B. and C. are creditors of D., A. an execution creditor, B. on D.'s covenant, and C. on D.'s promissory note. The sheriff levies on A.'s execution on D.'s goods, and claims the whole proceeds under his execution. What steps must C. and B. take to share in these proceeds?

A.—C. and B. can prove their claims under the Creditor's Relief Act, or get judgment in the regular way, and file a certificate under the Act, or issue writs of *fi. fa.* under the judgment, and place the same in the hands of the sheriff within one month from the entry of notice by the sheriff, and thus share ratably with A., but subject to his right to have the costs of the levy first paid.

(Compare Question, No. 19. *ante*.)

R. S. O., c. 65, s. 4.

35. Q.—A. wishes to sue B. on an account, the debit side of which is $450, while the credit side is $375, leaving $75 balance due. In what court must he sue? Why?

A.—The action must be brought in the County Court. It is not within the jurisdiction of the Division Court, for in that Court, no greater sum than $100 shall be recovered in any action for the balance of an unsettled account, nor shall any action for any such balance be sustained where the unsettled account in the whole exceeds $400.

R. S. O., c. 51, s. 77.

36. Q.—An action on a promissory note for $300 and interests and notarials by A.'s administrator C. against B. Draw statement of claim.

Q.A.—8

A.—In the County Court of the County of York,

Writ issued May 7th, A.D., 1890,

BETWEEN

C———, *Plaintiff,*

AND

B———, *Defendant.*

STATEMENT OF CLAIM.

(1). Letters of Administration of the estate of A., deceased, were granted on the 30th day of April, A.D., 1890, to C., jeweller of the City of Toronto, and the plaintiff herein.

(2) On the 1st day of April, A.D., 1890, the said B., the defendant herein, made a promissory note for the sum of $800 and interest, payable one month after date to the order of A.

(3) The said note became due and payable on Monday, the 5th day of May, A.D., 1890, and was presented and protested for non-payment.

The plaintiff claims :—

The amount of the note, together with interest thereon until judgment, and protest charges, and the costs of this action.

The plaintiff proposes that this action be tried at Toronto.

Delivered the 15th day of May, A.D., 1890.

By X. Y., plaintiff's solicitor.

87. Q.—A., the plaintiff, is suing to recover a cargo of oranges. B., the defendant, claims to hold them. A. knows B. to be worthless and also that if the oranges are not sold at once he will be a heavy loser. What steps can he take to have his rights protected ?

A.—Perishable articles may be sold under order of the Court or a Judge. If the application is made by the plaintiff it must be after the issue of the writ and on notice. If it is made by the defendant then it must be after appearance and on notice.

C. R. P., Nos. 1133 and 1134.

38. Q.—An action is brought by A. against B. on an open account set out in detail. B. appears to the writ and demands a statement of claim. A. moves for immediate judgment, and serves statement of claim. The judgment is refused, but time having in the meantime elapsed for delivery of statement of defence, and none being delivered, A., thereupon, signs judgment as for default of pleading. On the application of B. will the Court set the judgment aside ?

A.—Judgment by default may be set aside by the Court or a Judge upon such terms as to costs or otherwise as the Court or a Judge may think fit.

C. R. P., No. 796.

B. must file an affidavit showing the merits of the case, if any, and it must be shown that the plaintiff will not be subject to irreparable loss or injury.

39. Q.—A. is in a position to prove bribery againt B., a candidate elected to Parliament. In consideration of A.'s not prosecuting B., the latter makes a deed of a house and lot to A. B. subsequently seeks to have the deed cancelled. On what ground, if any, can he claim to have it set aside ?

A.—He can have it set aside on the ground that it is illegal.

40. Q.—A Charter party dated the 1st of June, contains
a covenant that a schooner shall proceed around Cobourg
to Charlotte on or before the 10th of June to take a load
of coal. The Charter party was not executed until the
11th of June, and the vessel sailed on the 15th of June.
How far will the owner be liable in an action for breach of
the contract by reason of the delay ?   Why ?

A.—Where the Charter party was not executed until
after the date for sailing the owner was only bound to sail
within a reasonable time. In this case in question he
sailed on the 15th, four days from the execution of the
Charter party, and if, from the circumstances of the case,
this is a reasonable time, then the owner would not be
liable in the action for breach of the contract.

41. Q.—A., of Toronto, being in London, asks his English correspondent B. to procure from C., at Liverpool,
certain bales of fine cloths, and ship along with certain
goods bought by A. from B. himself.   B. does so and sends
an invoice to A., which includes the goods bought from C.,
as well as those bought from B.   In consequence of defective packing the cloths are spoiled.   A. sues B. for the
damage.   How far can he make him liable ?

A.—B. is only a gratuitous agent, and as such he will
only be liable for gross negligence of packing.

42. Q.—A. is tenant under lease for four years unexpired.
B. is his landlord.   B. agrees to expend $250 in improve-
ment on the premises if A. will pay $50 per annum more
rent.   A. agrees verbally and B. expends the $250 as
agreed.   A. refuses to pay the extra rent and sets up as a
defence that the agreement was not written but verbal.
How far is the defence good ?   Why ?

A.—The defence is not good. This agreement does not require to be in writing because one of the parties can perform his part within the year.

43. Q.—Explain the difference between *executed* and *executory* considerations ?

A.—*Executed* consideration is already performed before the making of the promise, and this must have been at the request of the promissor, otherwise it will not support a promise. *Executory* consideration is not yet performed, and is to be done after the promise is made.

44. Q.—What is the difference between a factor and a broker ? How far does the difference between them affect the rights of third parties against the principal ?

A.—Factors are entrusted with the possession as well as the disposal of the property : while brokers are employed to contract about it, without being put into possession.

Smith, p. 118.

A factor can sell in his own name, and it is right that the principal should be bound by the consequences of such sale, as, for instance, the right of setting off a debt due from the factor. But the case of the broker is different ; he is not authorized to sell in his own name, and the vendee is not likely to be deceived because the broker has not the possession of the goods.

Smith, p. 167.

45. Q.—When are pleadings in an action deemed to be closed ?

A.—The pleadings are to be deemed closed on *joinder* being delivered, or on the expiration of the time for *reply*.

C. R. P., No. 392.

When the pleadings are closed, on default in delivery of pleading, this is to be noted by præcipe.

C. R. P., No. 893.

46. Q.—What are the consequences of disobeying an order for discovery ?

A.—If any party fails to comply with an order for production or inspection of documents he shall be liable to attachment. If a defendant he shall be liable to have his defence, if any, struck out, and to be placed in the same position as if he had not defended.

C. R. P., No. 520.

47. Q.—A plaintiff specially endorses a writ of summons. The defendant appears and demands a statement of claim. (a) What step may the plaintiff take equivalent to serving a statement of claim. (b) Draw what is necessary for the purpose in an action between B. and D.

A.—(a) The plaintiff may serve notice in lieu of statement of claim.

C. R. P., No. 370.

(b) H. C. J.—Q. B. D.

BETWEEN

A. B., *Plaintiff*,

AND

C. D., *Defendant*.

The particulars of the plaintiff's claim herein, and of the relief and remedy to which he claims to be entitled, appear by the endorsement of the Writ of Summons.

The plaintiff proposes that this action shall be tried at Toronto.

Dated at Toronto this —— day of —— A.D., 1890.

C. Y., Solicitor for plaintiff.

C. R. P., Form No. 16.

48. Q.—State the liabilities to third parties of a dormant partner in a concern.

A.—A dormant partner is liable to third parties so long as he remains a member of the firm. The third party must show that he is a partner.

49. Q.—A. and B. are in partnership. A. has separate estate apart from his interest in the partnership. C. is a creditor of the firm. D. is creditor of A. only. The firm fails, assets *nil*. A.'s estate is not sufficient to pay both C.'s and D.'s claim. Which has priority ?

A.—D. has priority. The separate estate of A. must be applied in payment of his separate creditors before any part can be taken by the partnership creditors. And partnership debts must be paid by the firm before the share of a deceased partner becomes available for his separate creditors.

Smith, p. 50.

50. Q.—A. is a broker to whom C. entrusts the possession of certain flannels. Hearing that A. is about to fail C. notifies A. that his employment is ended and demands his goods. A. does not give them up but disposes of them to B. C. claims them from B. Can he get them back ? Why ?

A.—No, he cannot get the goods back from B., because B. is not affected by the notice from C. to A.; but if B. had received notice himself it would have been different.

51. Q.—C. is arrested for debt. B., a friend of C., verbally promises C.'s creditor A. that he will pay C.'s debt if A. releases C. A. does so. Then B. refuses to pay on the ground that he did not promise in writing. How far is he right in his defence?

A.—In *Goodman v. Chase, 1 B. and Ald. 297*, the facts were the same, and the Court held the promise not within the statute, because the debt was gone by the discharge of the debtor out of custody.

Smith, pp. 570 and 571.

52. Q.—A. is captain of a schooner. B., the consignor in Toronto, ships by him to C. at Kingston a cargo of wheat said to contain 20,000 bushels. This quantity is mentioned in the bill of lading. The Bank of M. makes an advance to B. on the security of the bill of lading. It is discovered that there are only 15,000 bushels, which are not enough when sold to satisfy the advance. Who must bear the loss? Why?

A.—The Bank of M. stands in the same position as the consignee and can enforce the contract against the consignor. By the Bills of Lading Act, all rights of action, and liabilities upon the bill of lading, are to vest in and bind the consignee or endorsee to whom the property in the goods shall pass. And by the same Act the party signing the bill of lading may also be liable.

R. S. O., c. 122, s. 5, s-ss. 1 and 3.
Benjamin, p. 857.

53. Q.—Upon what material and at what stage of an action can you obtain the oral examination upon oath of a party to such action touching the matters in question therein ?

A.—Any party to an action or any person for whose immediate benefit an action is prosecuted or defended may be examined. If on the part of the plaintiff, it may take place at any time after the statement of defence of the party to be examined has been delivered, or after the time for delivery has expired. If on the part of the defendant it may take place after such defendant has delivered his statement of defence. The examination may be obtained on appointment and subpœna.

C. R. P., Nos. 487, 488 and 489.

54. Q.—On what material can you obtain a writ of replevin ?

A.—A writ of replevin is now abolished, but an order for replevin is obtainable on motion and affidavit, or præcipe and affidavit. When on præcipe, the affidavit must state that there is good reason to apprehend that, unless the order is issued without waiting for a motion, the delay would prejudice the rights of the claimant. The order is obtainable on præcipe and affidavit, if the property be distrained for rent or damage feasant.

C. R. P., Nos. 1098 and 1099.

55. Q.—Where one party refers to documents in a pleading, what right has the opposite party and what effect if refused ?

A.—The opposite party can give notice to produce, and, if refused, the party refusing will not be able to put such document in as evidence, unless he satisfies the Court that the document relates only to his own title, being a defendant, or that he had some other sufficient cause for not complying.

C. R. P., No. 514.

56. Q.—A. is assignee of an estate for the benefit of creditors. C., a creditor, files a claim which A. does not feel justified in admitting. What steps can the assignee take to compel C. to have his claim disposed of ?

A.—The assignee, or any person interested, may apply to the Judge of the County Court, on three days' notice to the creditor, and the Judge may order the creditor to prove his claim to the Judge's satisfaction within a time specified, and in default of so doing to be wholly barred.

R. S. O., c. 124, s. 20.

57. Q.—A. and B. are neighbors. B. has a cow which A. wants to buy. He asks B. if she is a good milker, and B. says, " She is; she gives ten quarts per day. You can take my word for it." A. next day buys the cow. He finds she is not what was represented, and seeks to repudiate the bargain. Can he do so ? Why ?

A.—No, this would not amount to a warranty. A representation in order to constitute a warrant must be made during the course of the dealing, and must enter into the bargain.

Benjamin, p. 605.

58. Q.—What modes are there of winding up joint stock companies? Explain briefly the procedure.

See R. S. O., c. 183.

59. Q.—What advances can an agent legally charge against the principal?

A.—He can charge all advances made by him in the regular course of his employment, for such the principal has impliedly required him to make.

Smith, p. 133.

60. Q.—Under what circumstances can a creditor legally claim interest on his claim against a debtor?

A.—He can claim interest from the time when a demand of payment is made in writing informing the debtor that interest will be charged from the date of demand.

R. S. O., c. 44, s. 86.

61. Q.—When goods are distrained for arrears of interest or rent, what notice of sale is required?

A.—The same notice as the landlord who distrains for rent is required to give.

R. S. O., c. 102, s. 17, s-s. 3.

62. Q.—A. executes a chattel mortgage to B. and subsequently assigns to C. for the benefit of all his creditors. E. and F. are execution creditors of A. with writs against goods in the sheriff's hands. What steps can be taken, and by whom, to contest the validity of B.'s chattel mortgage?

A.—The action must be brought by the assignee. But, however, on his default any creditor can get leave to do so.

R. S. O., c. 124, s. 7.

63. Q.—In a redemption suit, in default of payment according to the report, what right has the defendant ?

A.—The defendant is entitled to a final order for foreclosure against the plaintiff, or to an order dismissing the action with costs to be paid by the plaintiff to the defendant forthwith after taxation.

C. R. P., No. 362.

64. Q.—What is the position of a third party as to production of documents and examination, such third party having been brought into the action by a defendant, and having entered an appearance ?

A.—The position of the third party, who has been brought in by the defendant, is the same as the plaintiff and defendant in the action as regards production and examination, *i.e.*, the third party is like a defendant, and the defendant in the original action is like a plaintiff against the third party.

C. R. P., No. 509.

65. Q.—What is the general rule as to what facts must be pleaded by a party in an action ?

A.—Each party in any pleading must allege all such facts not appearing in the previous pleading (if any) as he means to rely on, and must raise all such grounds of defence or reply, as the case may be, as, if not so raised on the pleadings, would be likely to take the opposite party by surprise, or would raise new issues of fact not arising out of the pleadings ; as, for instance, fraud, or that any claim has been barred by a Statute of Limitations, or has been released.

C. R. P., No. 402.

66. Q.—On an assignment of a chose in action what effect has notice in writing to the original debtor of the fact of such assignment ?

A.—The effect is that the original debtor must pay the assignee after having received notice of the assignment ; and he will not be excused from such payment by paying it to his original creditor, *i.e.*, the assignor of the chose in action.

67. Q.—On a motion to dismiss for want of prosecution a plaintiff admits delay, but undertakes to speed the cause. Is this a sufficient answer to the motion ? Why ?

A.—No. This does not excuse the default, but as it is in the discretion of the Master he is often allowed to proceed on terms.

68. Q.—What is the difference between misjoinder and nonjoinder of parties to an action ? How cured ?

A.—Misjoinder is where the parties have been wrongly joined, but nonjoinder is where they have not been joined at all. Either can be cured by a motion to strike out or to add the parties.

C. R. P., Nos. 323 and 324.

69. Q.—In what different ways may there be a reference to the award of an arbitrator or referee ?

A.—The reference may be either by order of a Judge of the High Court, or of a Judge of the County Court, or it may be by voluntary submissions.

R. S. O., c. 53, ss. 1, 10 and 13.

70. Q.—What is the position of persons entitled to wages or salary where there is an assignment for benefit of creditors ?

A.—They have a priority over the rest of the creditors for three months' salary, and in respect of the balance, if any, they rank as ordinary creditors.

R. S. O., c. 127, s. 1.

71. Q.—A. is an endorser on a promissory note made by B. to C.   A. assigns to an assignee for the benefit of creditors.   What steps can C. take to file his claim against A.'s estate, the note not being due at the time of A.'s assignment ?

A.—C. can furnish to the assignee particulars of his claim proved by affidavit, and though his claim has not yet accrued due, he shall, nevertheless, be entitled to prove under the assignment, and vote at the meetings of creditors, but in ascertaining the amount of any such claim a deduction for interest shall be made for the time which has to run until the claim becomes due.   He should also place a value upon the security which he holds.

R. S. O., c. 124, s. 20.

72. Q.—In an action for replevin what bond may the defendant insist upon ?

A.—The defendant can insist on the sheriff getting a bond from two sureties in triple the value before he replevies.

C. R. P., No. 1103.

73. Q.—How may process or summons be served on a corporation (a) in Superior Court and (b) Division Court actions ?

A.—(a) See C. R. P., No. 267.

(b) See R. S. O., c. 51, s. 101.

74. Q.—B., a merchant from London, Ontario, buys in Quebec from A. a lot of damaged woollens. He pays A. by note at thirty days. The goods are shipped to B. but before they arrive in London A. learns that B. is insolvent. What right has A., the note not being matured, but having been discounted by him before learning of his insolvency ?

A.—A. can stop the goods *in transitu*. The note was not taken as an absolute payment, and the fact that A. had discounted it does not signify, unless he discounted it in such a way as not to be liable on it himself.

Benjamin, p. 822.

75. Q.—A. agrees to become a surety for the dealings of B. with the firm C. D. & Co. At the time of the arreement the firm is composed of C. D. & E. E. dies and F. takes his place, but the firm's name is unchanged. How far does A. continue liable after the change ?

A.—Where a security, which is intended to continue in force notwithstanding any change that may take place in its constitution, is given to the firm, such intent must appear, either expressly or by implication, upon the security; since otherwise it will become inoperative as to future events on the incoming or outgoing of a partner. The same rule is applied to contracts under seal and simple contracts.

> *Berclay* v. *Lucas, 1 T. R. 291.*
> *Strange* v. *Lee, 3 East 484.*
> Smith, pp. 55 and 56.

——— ———

(N.B.—There have been excluded from the above collection twenty-one repeated questions.—F. L. W.)

PART II.

CALL TO THE BAR.

CALL TO THE BAR.

CHAPTER V.

REAL PROPERTY AND WILLS.

1. Q.—A. purchases at a sale a house described in the particulars as a brick built house. He pays his deposit; but, before completion of the contract, he discovers that the house is in fact a rough-cast house veneered with brick. Can A. recover his deposit? Why? Would it make any difference if A. had looked at the house before bidding at the sale? Why?

A.—A. can rescind the contract and recover the deposit because it does not answer the description. If he saw the house and noticed that it was not according to description he could not then recover the deposit; but if the defect was not apparent it would not make any difference whether he saw it or not.

Dart, p. 138.

2. Q.—A contract for the sale of land names a day for its completion. No agreement is made as to interest on the purchase money. When will the purchaser be liable for interest:—(1) Where he is out of possession? (2) Where he is in possession?

A.—(1) The purchaser, if out of possession, is liable for interest if the delay beyond the day set to close is caused by himself, but he is not liable if the delay is caused by the vendor.

(2) If the purchaser is in possession he is liable for interest in either case.

Re Dingman and Hall, C. L. J., June, 1890.

3. Q.—Explain the doctrine of tacking. Is it in force in Ontario ?

A.—Tacking is the process by which a mortgagee may, by taking a further mortgage for a further advance upon the same property, defeat the equitable claims of a *mesne* incumbrancer, *i.e.*, a person who has lent money on the property after the first but before the further mortgage. The tacking mortgagee gains this right by virtue of his legal title under the first mortgage, and by the operation of the rule that where the equities (as that under the second and third mortgage) are equal the law shall prevail.

Wharton's Law Lexicon, p. 718.

Tacking has been abolished in Ontario by R. S. O., c. 114, s. 83, in so far as it interferes with the registered title.

The result of this is that tacking may take place apart from the Registry Act, but as against that enactment it shall not prevail.

Armour, p. 62.

4. Q.—What is meant by disclaimer of tenure ?

A.—Disclaimer of tenure is a renunciation, or a denial by a tenant of his landlord's title, either by refusing to pay rent, denying any obligation to pay, or by setting up a

liable for
is caused
ed by the

for inter-

)0.

n force in

agee may,
ance upon
of a *mesne*
ey on the
mortgage.
tue of his
operation
under the
all prevail.

. O., c. 114,
l title.
place apart
inactment it

e ?

a denial by
ing to pay
:tting up a

title in himself or a third person, and this is a distinct
ground for forfeiture of the lease or other tenancy.

Wharton's Law Lexicon, p. 237.

5. Q.—The Bank of Montreal will please pay to A. B.
$1000 at the expiration of a month after my death.

Witness C. D.,   " J. S."

What is the nature of this instrument and what is its
effect ?

A.—This instrument is testamentary in form, and is
imperfect for want of proper attestation, and is therefore
ineffectual. In *Mitchell* v. *Smith, 12 W. R. 941*, it was
decided that, if the donor intends to make a testamentary
gift which turns out to be ineffectual, that gift will not be
supported as a *donatio mortis causa*, notwithstanding that
there was a complete delivery.

Snell, p. 194.

6. Q.—What is the effect of a devise " to A. and his
children " : (1) Where A. has children living at the date of
the will ?   (2) Where he has no children living at the date
of the will ?

A.—(1) Where A. has children living at the date of the
will the words " his children " are not construed as words
of limitation ; hence, A. and his children will take as
tenants in common.

(2) Where no children are living at the date of the will
it will be construed as a devise to A. in fee tail.

Theobald, p. 334.

7. Q.—A purchaser of land, being informed by the vendor as to the title, lays the fact before counsel who approves

of the title, and advises the purchaser to accept it.   Is the counsel responsible in case of a defect?

A.—Yes, he is liable in Ontario, but in England it is otherwise, for there his services are only deemed to be honorary.

8. Q.—A devise to A. for life and after his death to his issue. A. dies in the lifetime of the testator. What becomes of the land which is the subject of the devise ?

A.—It will not lapse but will be deemed to take effect as if A. died immediately after the testator.

R. S. O., c. 109, s. 35.

9. Q.—Define and distinguish between *satisfaction* and *ademption*.

A.—*Satisfaction* only arises between a gift and a prior liability to give, and not between a sum actually settled and a subsequent gift by will or otherwise. When there is a gift by will to a child and the testator afterwards in his lifetime gives the child a sum of money the gift is *ademed*.

Theobald, p. 586.

Ademption is revocation ; it is a taking away of a legacy, *i.e.*, if a testator, after having given a legacy by his will, alienate the subject of it during his life, it is an *ademption.*

Wharton's Law Lexicon, p. 19.

10. Q.—A devise is made to A. of Whiteacre subject to an annuity payable thereout to B., his executors and administrators. (*a*) What is the nature of B.'s interest ? (*b*) What remedies has he for the recovery of his money if

it is not paid ? (c) Upon whom does his interest devolve
on his death intestate ?

A.—(a) B. takes a perpetual annuity.

(b) He can either sue for the annuity, or he can proceed
against the land to recover it.

(c) On B.'s death his interest will devolve upon his personal representatives.

11. Q.—Is a copy of a deed certified by a registrar
admissible in evidence instead of the original deed ?   If so,
under what circumstances and with what effect ?

A.—A copy of a deed certified by a registrar is *prima
facie* evidence, if ten days' notice of intention to produce
such is given.   But if the opposite party objects he will
have to produce the original instrument.

Armour, pp. 86 and 87.

12. Q.—At a sale by a first mortgagee under a power
contained in his mortgage the mortgagor buys. (a) Does
he take the land freed from a second mortgage created by
him ?   (b) If a stranger buys at the sale and the mortgagor subsequently buys *bona fide* from him, does he take
the land freed from a second mortgage created by himself?

A.—(a) No. (b) No. This has been set aside on the
ground of fraud. *Faulds* v. *Harper*, in the Court of Appeal
for Ontario, is a late case in point.

13. Q.—When is an abstract of title said to be perfect?

A.—When the abstract, commencing with a good root
and continuing down to contract, shows that the vendor can

convey the legal and equitable estates in the land, it is said
to be a perfect abstract.

Armour, p. 89.

14. Q.—Who are the proper parties defendant to an
action of specific performance by the purchaser of land,
where the vendor has died intestate after contract but before conveyance and payment of the purchase money?

A.—The personal representatives are the proper persons
to be defendants in the action. If none are appointed then
the plaintiff can apply to the Court to have some one
appointed for the purposes of the action.

15. Q.—A. is the highest bidder at a judicial sale of land
and the Master makes a report declaring him to be the
purchaser. Before the report is filed the buildings on the
land, which were uninsured, are burned. Is the purchaser
bound to complete his purchase? If so, must he pay the
full purchase money? Why?

A.—The purchaser is bound to complete his purchase,
but the property will not pass to him until the report has
been confirmed, and, therefore, he will not be compelled to
bear the loss occasioned by the fire, and a deduction in the
price will have to be made to cover this loss.

16. Q.—A testator bequeaths to A. B. a specific horse.
It is found after the death of the testator that the horse is
subject to a chattel mortgage. Is A. B. entitled to have
the mortgage paid out of the general estate?

A.—Yes, A. B. is entitled to have the mortgage paid out
of general estate, if it is sufficient, for the general personal
estate is primarily liable for debts.

17. Q.—Explain the doctrine of conversion and state the essentials of conversion by will.

A.— That money directed to be employed in the purchase of realty, and realty directed to be sold and turned into money, are considered in equity as that species of property into which they are directed to be converted.   The direction must be imperative, and in a will speaks from the death of the testator, and in a deed from the date of the deed or from the time specified in the deed.

18. Q.—(1) A devise to A. B. and the heirs of his body on condition that he shall not marry.   (2) A devise to the testator's widow provided she shall not marry again. Construe these.

A.—(1) This is not a valid restraint and A. B. will not lose the devise if he marries.

(2) This is a valid restraint, if the testator chooses to impose it, and if the widow marries again she will lose the devise.

19. Q.—What is the general rule as to the construction of conditions of sale ?

A.—Conditions of sale are construed strictly against the vendor and in favour of the vendee.

Armour, p. 7.

20. Q.—What matters are essential to make an agreement for the sale of land valid under the Statute of Frauds ?

A.—The Statute of Frauds enacts that " no action shall be brought on any contract or sale of lands, tenements, or

hereditaments, or any interest in or concerning them, unless the agreement, upon which such action shall be brought
or some memorandum or note thereof, shall be in writing
and signed by the party to be charged therewith, or some
other person thereunto by him lawfully authorized."

Pollock, pp. 221 and 223.

21. Q.—A purchaser who has been furnished with an
abstract is satisfied with the title abstracted except as to
one point:—The construction of a will. His solicitor at
his request makes out a case for the opinion of counsel,
stating that his client is satisfied with the title subject to
his opinion on the will. The opinion is favorable to the
purchaser. He then becomes dissatisfied with the proof of
a pedigree and so informs the vendor. The latter, having
heard of the opinion of counsel, insists upon the purchaser
adhering to his satisfaction with the title as expressed in
the case submitted to counsel. Is the purchaser bound
thereby? Reason.

A.—The purchaser is not bound thereby because he has
not waived any objection to the title which he may choose
to make as between himself and the vendor.

Armour, p. 20.

22. Q.—What is the effect of a mortgage in fee simple by
a tenant in tail and statutory discharge thereof?

A.—The discharge acts as a re-conveyance of the fee,
and, therefore, the tenant in tail becomes the owner in fee,
and the entailment as defeated.

Leith, p. 514.

23. Q.—Whose duty is it to prepare the conveyance on a sale of lands in the absence of special conditions ? Who bears the expense of preparing, and who bears the expense of getting it executed ?

A.—It is the purchaser's duty to prepare the deed and bear the expense thereof, and it is the vendor's duty to get it executed and bear the expense of the same.

24. Q.—Under what circumstances may recitals in deeds be relied upon as evidence ?

A.—Recitals in deeds 20 years old at the date of the contract are, unless and except so far as they are proved to be inaccurate, to be taken to be sufficient evidence of the truth of such facts, matters and descriptions.

Armour, p. 90.

25. Q.—(1) A devise to A. for life and after his death to his heirs and the heirs female of their bodies. (2) A devise to A. for life and after his death to his heirs, their heirs and assigns, forever. What does A. take in each case ?

A.—(1) A. takes a life estate with remainder in special tail to his heirs. The rule in Shelley's case is excluded by the narrowing of the course of descent. (2) In this case the rule in Shelley's case applies and A. will take a fee simple.

26. Q.—What is meant by conversion ? How is it affected and if at all by recent legislation ?

A.—See Question No. 17 ante.

It is now affected by the Devolution of Estates Act, which enacts that all property devolves upon the personal representatives.

27. Q.—When two clauses in a will are absolutely irreconcilable which is to be preferred ?

A.—The latter clause is to be preferred in a will, because it was written later by the testator, and he must have been presumed to have intended it to take effect rather than the former clause.

28. Q.—After conveyance has a purchaser any recourse if he discovers encumbrances concealed by the vendor ? What are his rights?

A.—If the vendor is guilty of any fraud an action would lie at the suit of the vendee, but otherwise the vendee would have no recourse, except in the case of covenants in the conveyance by the vendor, and then only on those covenants.

29. Q.—Is it necessary to abstract discharged mortgages and expired leases in preparing an abstract?

A.—The abstract should show in chronological order every devolution of the estate by deed, will, or other instrument, or by inheritance, including all incumbrances, whether discharged or existing, but excluding leases which have expired by effluxion of time.

Prideaux on Conveyancing, p. 139.
Armour, p. 85.

30. Q.—In proving title between vendor and purchaser what is sufficient evidence of discharged mortgages when they cannot be produced by the vendor ?

A.—When the purchaser is entitled to evidence of facts not established by the deeds, and not of such a nature as to be susceptible of proof by official certificates, they may be proven by statutory declarations. In the case of discharged mortgages the registered memorials shall be sufficient unless they are proved to be inaccurate ; and the vendor shall not be bound to produce the mortgages unless they are in his possession or power.

Armour, p. 95.

R. S. O., c. 112, s. 1, s-s. 2.

31. Q.—State some of the modes in which a purchaser may waive his right to have a good title proved.

A.—The purchaser may waive his right by taking possession of the property, or offering it for sale, or otherwise dealing with it as if it were his own.

32. Q.—Give an instance of a devise for life with remainder to heirs to which the rule in Shelley's case does not apply.

A.—In cases of marriage settlements the rule in Shelley's case will not be followed, for the Court always construes them strictly in favour of the persons intended.

33. Q.—What is the effect of the Devolution of Estates Act, 1886, upon a specific devise of Real Estate.

A.—Now by the Devolution of Estates Act all property passes to the personal representatives as personalty, and after the debts have been paid they can then be called upon to convey the estate to the devisee.

34. Q.—What is the effect of the usual recital in the body of a conveyance that the purchase money has been paid ?

A.—It shall be a sufficient discharge to the person paying or delivering the same, and shall, in favour of a subsequent purchaser, not having notice that the money or
other consideration, thereby acknowledged to be received,
was not in fact paid or given wholly or in part, be sufficient
evidence of the payment or giving of the whole amount
thereof.

R. S. O., c. 100, s. 6.

In *Barber* v. *McKay, C. L. J. 1890*, it was held that
the man with a paper title must prove consideration, as
against a trespasser in possession, who had an unregistered
title.

(N. B.—Thirty-seven questions have been excluded from
this list in consequence of having been repeated either in
this collection or in the collection on Real Property and
Wills in Part I.—F. L. W.)

CHAPTER VI.

HARRIS, BROOM, BLACKSTONE.

1. Q.—What is the difference between *larceny* and *embezzlement* by a clerk or servant? Explain by example.

A.—*Larceny* is the wilfully wrongful taking possession of the goods of another with the intent to deprive the owner of his property in them.

Embezzlement is the unlawful appropriation to his own use by a servant or clerk of money or chattels received by him for and on account of his master or employer. The latter is committed in respect of property which is not at the time in the actual or legal possession of the owner, but in the former the property is in the owner's possession.

Examples.—A clerk takes $10 from his master's till; this is *larceny*. A clerk receives $10 in payment for goods sold by his master and appropriates it to his own use; this is *embezzlement*.

2. Q.—If two persons commit perjury in an affidavit made by them jointly and severally, can they be indicted jointly therefor, or must they be indicted separately?

A.—They cannot be indicted jointly because the offence does not admit of being committed jointly.

Harris, p. 384.

3. Q.—What is the main distinction in regard to the remedy against a Magistrate who acts erroneously within his jurisdiction?

A.—The main distinction to be noted in regard to the remedy available against a Magistrate who acts without jurisdiction, and that available against a Magistrate who acts erroneously within his jurisdiction, is thus pointed out by Mr. Justice Erle :—"If the act of the Magistrate is done *without jurisdiction* it is a trespass; if *within the jurisdiction*, the action rests upon the corruptness of motive, and to establish this the act must be shown to be malicious."

Broom, p. 803.

4. Q.—Give an example of the crime of obtaining money or goods by false pretences where the false pretence is not expressed in words.

A.—An example of the crime as stated would be the case of a man obtaining goods by giving his cheque for them, knowing that the cheque would not be honored when presented.

5. Q.—Is a lunatic answerable for his torts ?

A.—Even a lunatic will be civilly answerable for his torts although he may be wholly incapable of design. This is founded upon the general principle that whenever one person receives an injury or bodily hurt directly from the voluntary act of another, that is a trespass, although there was no design to injure.

Broom, p. 753.

6. Q.—In an action of libel will the fact that the defendant has published of the plaintiff other libels than the one complained of be admissible in evidence for the plaintiff ? If so, for what purpose ?

A.—Evidence of other libels will be admissible to show the intent.

l to the
without
ate who
nted out
e is done
jurisdic-
tive, and
cious."

7. Q.—Define *corporations aggregate* and *sole*. Give an example of the latter and explain the object of the creation of that kind of corporation.

A.—*Corporations aggregate* consist of many members, while *corporations sole* consist of one member only. Here, an example of a *corporation sole* is the Crown, and, in England, a Bishop. The object is to have some one to represent property and to enter into contracts in regard thereto.

ig money
ice is not

8. Q.—What is the difference between *robbery* and *assault with intent to rob?*

A.—*Robbery* is the felonious and forcible taking from the person of another, or in his presence against his will of any money or goods to any value by violence or putting him to fear.

the case
for them,
hen pre-

Assault with intent to rob is an attempt or offer to commit a forcible crime against the person of another with intent to rob. It is a misdemeanor punishable by imprisonment not exceeding two years. If the intent be not proven the defendant may in that case be convicted of a common assault.

e for his
gn. This
iever one
from the
igh there

9. Q.—Who can be bail?

A.—The magistrate (or Court) will act according to his discretion as to the sufficiency of the bail. The proposed bail may be examined upon oath as to their means, though in criminal cases no justification of bail is required. A married woman, an infant, a prisoner in custody, or a person who has been convicted of an infamous crime, as perjury, cannot be bail.

ie defend-
n the one
plaintiff?

e to show

Harris, p. 320.
Q.A.—10

10. Q.—When is a principal liable for the publication of libel by a servant?

A.—The principal is always liable for the publication of a libel by his servant, unless the servant acts beyond his authority.

11. Q.—What is the distinction between *crimes* and *offences* in the narrower signification of these terms?

A.—In the narrower signification of these terms *crimes* may be said to be acts which are the subject of indictment, and *offences* may be said to be those acts which are not indictable but which are punished on a summary conviction.

12. Q.—When can several prisoners be jointly indicted and tried together, and what is the law in regard to the admissibility of the evidence of one of them or of the wife of one of them for or against the other?

A.—When several persons take part in the commission of an offence, they may all be indicted together, or any number of them together, or each separately; and of course some may be convicted and others acquitted. But certain offences do not admit of a joint commission, as for example, *perjury*. This joinder of defendants may be made the subject of demurrer, motion in arrest of judgment, or writ of error; or the Court will in general quash the indictment.

Harris, p. 384.

As to the evidence of one of them, or the wife of one of them, for or against the other, the rule is that it is not admissible; but if one is acquitted his evidence then becomes admissible.

13. Q.—Under what circumstances may one person be held liable for a trespass committed by another on the ground of ratification ?

A.—The doctrine of "*ratihabitio*" is of more difficult application in reference to torts than in reference to contracts. If A., *professing to act by my authority* does that which *prima facie* amounts to a trespass, and I afterwards assent to and adopt his act, then he is treated as having from the beginning acted by my authority, and I become a trespasser, unless I can *justify* the particular act which is to be deemed as having been done with my previous sanction. In this case the party ratifying becomes, as it were, a trespasser *by estoppel*; at all events, he is precluded from denying that he gave antecedent authority for that act which he afterwards admits himself to have authorized. In *Wilson* v. *Tumman*, *2 M. & Gr. 236, 242-3*, the rule under notice is fully and elaborately stated in these words :—
"That an act done *for another* by a person not assuming to act for himself but for such other person, though without any antecedent authority whatever, becomes the act of the principal, if subsequently ratified by him, is the known and well established rule of law. In that case the principal is bound by the act, whether it be for his detriment or his advantage, and whether it be founded on a tort or a contract, to the same extent as by—and with all the consequences which follow from—the same act done by his previous authority." The judgment in *Buron* v. *Denman* noticed in Broom's Common Law at pages 101, and 773, and the cases there cited, should be examined in connection with this subject.

Broom, pp. 847, 771 *et seq.*

14. Q.—In what cases may an action of slander be maintained *without proof of special damage?*

A.—In order to sustain an action for slander *without proof of special damage,* evidence must be given of some imputation on the plaintiff of a crime punishable by law, or of the having some contagious disorder which may exclude from society, or the words complained of must be shown to have been spoken of the plaintiff with reference to his trade, office, or profession, and to have been calculated to injure him therein.

Broom, p. 880.

15. Q.—What effect has the death of a Sovereign on the continuance of Parliament at common law ; and how does the law now stand by Statute?

A.—At common law the death of the Sovereign had the effect of a dissolution of Parliament; but by Statute no Parliament of Canada is dissolved in consequence of the demise of the Crown.

R. S. C., c. 11, s. 1.

16. Q.—What is the test as to whe[...] seditious wo[...]s are innocent or not?

A.—The test proposed by an eminent authority is :— " Has the communication a plain tendency to produce public mischief by perverting the mind of the subject and creating a general dissatisfaction towards government ?"

17. Q.—On a criminal trial is the fact that the accused was intoxicated when the offence was committed material in any case? If so, in what way?

A.—Voluntary intoxication is no excuse for crime. It is sometimes taken into consideration, however, and it is sometimes the indication of the quality of an act. It may be taken into account by the jury when considering the motive or intent of a person acting under its influence.

Harris, pp. 25 and 26.

18. Q.—Under what circumstances is the evidence of the prisoner's good character important on a criminal trial? By what sort of evidence is such a character proved and how may it be rebutted?

A.—" Judges frequently tell juries that evidence of character cannot be used when the case is clearly proved except in mitigation (or possibly aggravation) of punishment; but if they have any doubt evidence of character is highly important." Witnesses may be called to speak generally as to the good character of the prisoner. This general evidence of good character may be disproved by general evidence of bad character; but not by particular cases of misconduct. For such purposes previous convictions may as a rule be proved.

Harris, p. 415.

19. Q.—Explain what is meant by a *trespasser ab initio*.

A.—Where a man misdemeans himself, or makes an illuse of the authority with which the law intrusts in him, he shall be accounted a *trespasser ab initio*; as if one come into a tavern and will not go out in a reasonable time, but tarries there all night contrary to the inclinations of the owner, this wrongful act shall affect and have relation back even to his first entry, and make the whole a trespass; but a bare non-feasance, as not paying for the wine he calls for, will not make him a trespasser, for this is only a breach of contract.

Harris, p. 846.

20. Q.—Give an example of a tort flowing from a breach of contract.

A.—Solicitors or Doctors or Engineers undertake to discharge their duties with a reasonable amount of skill, and with integrity. For any neglect or unskilfulness on their part, a party who has been injured thereby may maintain an action either *in tort* for the wrong done or *in contract* at his election.

Broom, p. 740.

21. Q.—Explain the law as to the necessity for proof of malice in an action of libel.

A.—Mere publication of matter, which on the face of it is libellous, is presumptive evidence of malice, which is necessary to constitute a crime; therefore, proof of innocence of intention lies on the defendant. But if the writing is *prima facie* innocent, malice may be proved from special circumstances, which may be laid before the jury.

Harris, p. 111.

22. Q.—When can evidence of particular acts of conduct be given?

A.—Evidence of particular acts of conduct may be given when it tends directly to the disproving of some of the facts put in issue by the pleadings.

23. Q.—When is one witness sufficient in perjury?

A.—The general rule is that two are required, or one and another to corroborate his testimony; but the rule does

not apply when the perjury consists in the defendant having contradicted what he swore to on oath on a former
occasion.

Harris, p. 84.

24. Q.—Of what consequence is the absence of actual
malice in an action of libel?

A.—In order to constitute a libel it is necessary that there
should be actual malice. This is sometimes presumed and
at other times it is necessary to prove it. If the occasion
is privileged then actual malice will not be presumed but
must be proved.

(Compare Question No. 21 *ante*.)
Harris, pp. 101 and 107.

25. Q.—Explain the difference between the actions of
malicious arrest and *false imprisonment*.

A.—*Malicious arrest* is the putting in force the process
of the law maliciously and without reasonable and pro-
bable cause. In this the *onus* is on the plaintiff.

In *false imprisonment* there are two requisites—the
detention of the person, and the unlawfulness of such
detention. The *onus* in this case is on the defendant.

Broom, p. 811.

26. Q.—To what action or actions is a man liable who
commits a battery upon a married woman?

A.—He is liable, at the instance of the married woman,
for an assault and for damages; and he is liable, at the
instance of the husband, for damages for the loss of his
wife's company, society, etc.

27. Q.—What is a good defence to an action for *battery?*

A.—It is a good defence to an action for *battery* if it is committed in self-defence, or in moderate correction, or in the execution of public justice, or in some lawful game.

Harris, p. 181.

28. Q.—Should the Court construe strictly or liberally Penal Acts and Acts against fraud respectively? Is there any apparent inconsistency in the rules governing such construction, and if so, how do you reconcile them?

A.—Generally Statutes are construed by the "Golden Rule," as it is legally termed; but Penal Statutes are construed strictly, and if there is any doubt the Court will always lean against the construction which imposes a burden on the subject, and give the prisoner the benefit of the doubt. This apparent inconsistency is accounted for by the principle that the Court will not punish a subject until he is clearly proven to be guilty, and the authority for such punishment, as well as the facts of the case, must be without doubt.

Broom, pp. 6 and 7.

29. Q.—What is the effect of consent in assault?

A.—As a rule consent on the part of the complainant deprives the act of the character of an assault, unless, indeed, non-resistance has been brought about by fraud. But the fact of consent will in general be immaterial when an actual battery or breach of the peace has been committed.

Harris, p. 180.

30. Q.—Explain briefly the meaning of the maxim " *respondeat superior.*"

A.—*" Respondeat superior "—Let the principal be held responsible.* The person directing an unlawful act to be done by his servant or agent is answerable as if he had done the act with his own hand.

Wharton's Law Lexicon, p. 640.

31. Q.—Define and explain briefly *malice in law* and *malice in fact* respectively.

A.—*Malice in law* is where a wrongful act is done intentionally without just cause or excuse.

Malice in fact is said to be of two kinds, viz :—Personal malice against the individual, and that sort of general disregard of the right consideration due to all mankind which, indeed, may not be previously directed against any one, but is nevertheless productive of injury to the complainant.

Broom, p. 805.

32. Q.—What is the difference, as regards their effect upon the issue of a marriage, between a divorce on the ground of corporal deformity at the time of marriage, and a divorce on some ground arising after the marriage?

A.—The issue in the first case will be deemed *bastards*, but in the second case they will be *legitament*.

33. Q.—What is the difference between *nonfeasance* and *misfeasance* of a gratuitous service as regards the liability of the party undertaking it ?

A.—A person who offers a gratuitous service is liable for *misfeasance* but not for *nonfeasance*. As, for instance, if a man offers gratuitously to insure a house for another, he will be liable if he does it wrongly, but he will not be liable if he does not do it at all.

84. Q.—Explain the meaning of *treasure-trove* and state briefly when it belongs to the Crown and when to an individual.

A.—*Treasure-trove* is money or coin, gold, silver, plate, or bullion found hidden in the earth or other private place, the owner thereof being unknown or unfound; in which case it belongs to the Crown.

If it is found *on* the ground, and the owner thereof is unknown or unfound, it then belongs to the individual finding it.

> Wharton's Law Lexicon, p. 735.
> Harris, p. 70.

(N.B.—From this collection their have been excluded eighty-seven questions, a few of which were repetitions; but the majority of them were excluded in consequence of their having been answered in "Robert's Questions and Answers on Criminal Law."—F.L.W.)

CHAPTER VII.

BYLES, BEST, POLLOCK.

1. Q.—To what extent will gross negligence of a plaintiff in taking a bill or note payable to bearer, and for which he has given consideration, be a defence to an action brought by him.

A.—Formerly the negligence of the plaintiff would be a good defence. But it is now settled that if a man take *honestly* an instrument made, or become payable to bearer, he has a good title to it, with whatever degree of negligence he may have acted, unless his gross negligence induce the jury to find fraud. Gross negligence only would not be a sufficient answer by the defendant where the plaintiff has given consideration for the bill. Gross negligence may be evidence of *mala fides*, but it is not the same thing.

Byles, pp. 187 and 188.

2. Q.—A bill is drawn at 3 months, dated 29th Jan., 1886, and duly accepted. State accurately the time at which the acceptor is bound to pay, and when a holder is entitled to treat the bill as dishonored.

A.—The acceptor is bound to pay on May 2nd, 1884, unless that be Sunday or a legal holiday, and unless paid by 3 o'clock on May 2nd, the holder is entitled to treat the bill as dishonored and proceed to protest it.

3. Q.—A. is induced, by a fraudulent misrepresentation of the nature of the instrument, to sign his name to a

promissory note. To what extent, if at all, is he liable to an innocent holder for value ?

A.—He never intended to sign the note and therefore in contemplation of law never did sign it, (however, A. may be estopped from disputing it if there be negligence on his part). There is no exception to this rule in favor of *bona fide* holders of negotiable instruments.

Pollock, pp. 456-459.

4. Q.—What is the effect of an agreement between A. and B. that B. should do certain work, and that A. should pay him for it whatever he (A.) should think reasonable ?

A.—In *Roberts* v. *Smith, 4 H. & N. 315,* the facts were the same, and the Court held that there was no contract which could be enforced. Services had indeed been rendered, and of the sort for which people usually are paid and expect to be paid ; so that in the absence of an express agreement there would have been a good cause of action for a reasonable reward. But here the plaintiff had expressly assented to take whatever the defendant should think reasonable (which might be nothing), and had thus precluded himself from claiming to have whatever a jury should think reasonable. It would not be safe, however, to infer from this case that under no circumstances whatever can a promise to give what the promisor shall think reasonable amount to a promise to give a reasonable reward, or at all events something which can be found as a fact to be illusory. The circumstances of each case (or in a written instrument the context) must be looked to for the real meaning of the parties, and it is only when the illusory promise reserves an unlimited option to the promisor that the contract gives no right of action to the person who has performed the service.

Pollock, pp. 117 and 118.

5. Q.—Is there any, and if so, what difference between the liability of a *trading* and a *non-trading corporation* on contracts not under seal ?

A.—All contracts by *trading corporations* entered into for the purposes for which they are incorporated are valid and binding upon the company though not under seal. *Necessary* and *incidental* contracts by *non-trading corporations* may be made without seal.

Pollock, pp. 212 *et seq.*

6. Q.—" Sometimes even when the thing which is the subject-matter of an agreement is specifically ascertained, the agreement may be avoided by material error as to some attribute of the thing." Under what circumstances will error of this kind suffice to make the transaction void ?

A.—An error of this kind will not suffice to make the contract void unless—

(1) It is such that according to the ordinary course of dealing and use of language the difference made by the absence of the quality wrongly supposed to exist amounts to a difference in kind ;

(2) And the error is also common to both parties.

Example : The sale of a *golden* vessel which proves only to be brass. The object of their common intention is not merely this specific vessel, but this specific vessel, *being golden.* Then, and not otherwise, the sale is void.

Pollock, pp. 478 and 479.

7. Q.—State exceptions to the rule requiring the personal attendance of witnesses at trials.

A.—The rule is that "a person who without just cause absents himself from a trial at which he has been duly summoned to attend as a witness is liable to punishment for contempt." The only exception to this is that of the Sovereign, against whom no compulsory process can issue.

The Court or a Judge may order affidavits to be read in certain cases, or may order certain witnesses to be exam·ined by interrogatories or otherwise.

Best, pp. 139 and 174.

8. Q.—Under what circumstances will evidence of char·acter of litigant parties be admissible ?

A.—The general rule is that it is not receivable, but there is an exception to this when the character of a party is in issue by the proceedings, as in actions for seduction, rape, and the like.

Best, pp. 357 and 358.

9. Q.—Mention and give examples of the different kinds of *estoppel*.

A.—(1) *Estoppels by matter of record :* As letters-patent, pleading, judgment, etc.

(2) *Estoppels by deed :* As special recitals.

(3) *Estoppels in pais :* As acts of notoriety not less formal and solemn than the execution of a deed, such as livery, entry, acceptance of an estate, etc.

Best, pp. 678 *et seq.*

10. Q.—When a plaintiff delivers a *replication* to which it is necessary for the defendant to plead new facts not already pleaded, how is this to be done ?

A.—No pleading subsequent to *reply*, other than a *joinder of issue*, shall be pleaded without leave of the Court or a Judge, and then upon such terms as the Court or Judge thinks fit.

C. R. P., No. 882.

11. Q.—Can an infant enforce his voidable contracts against the other party to them during his infancy? State exceptions to the rule.

A.—As a general rule an infant can enforce his voidable contracts; but an infant cannot have specific performance because the remedy is not mutual, the infant not being bound; and an infant cannot recover the money he has paid on a contract which has been wholly or partly performed by the other party.

Pollock, pp. 131 and 132.

12. Q.—When a party contracts with an agent whom he does not know to be an agent, to what extent is the undisclosed principal bound by and entitled to enforce the contract?

A.—Where the agent is not known to be agent the undisclosed principal is generally bound by the contract and entitled to enforce it. But the limitations of this rule are important. It does not apply where an agent for an undisclosed principal contracts in such terms as import that he is the real and only principal. Nor does it apply if the nature of the contract itself (as partnership) were inconsistent with a principal unknown at the time taking the place of the apparent contracting party. Or if the principal represents the agent as principal he is bound by that representation. So if he stands by and allows a third

person innocently to treat with the agent as principal he
cannot afterwards turn round and sue him in his own
name.   Where the rule does apply the principal must take
the contract subject to all equities in the same way as if
the agent were the sole principal.

Pollock, p. 168-170.

13. Q.—To what extent is a promise of forbearance to
sue a good consideration for a contract ?

A.—The forbearance to sue must be for a definite or
ascertainable time.   Forbearance for a reasonable time is
enough, for it can be ascertained, as a question of fact,
what is a reasonable time in any given case.   "Forbearance
to press for immediate payment" may be construed by help
of the circumstances and context as meaning forbearance
for a reasonable time.   There must be an actual or *bona
fide* disputed right.

Pollock, p. 244.

14. Q.—Where a difference of local laws is in question,
by what law is the lawfulness of a contract to be determined ?

A.—The *lex loci contractus* must govern; unless it is to
be performed in another country, when the *lex loci solutionis*
will govern.

Pollock, pp. 887 and 688.

15. Q.—Under what circumstances is probate evidence
of a will in actions concerning real estate?

A.—Probate of the will, or letters of administration with
the will annexed, properly stamped with the Surrogate
Court seal is *prima facie* evidence of such will.   Ten days

notice must be given to the opposite party of intention to use it as proof. This shall be sufficient evidence unless within four days after notice is received the other party gives notice that he disputes the validity of the devise or other testamentary disposition.

R. S. O., c. 61, s. 88.

16. Q.—Give exceptions to the rule that the law allows no excuse for withholding evidence which is relevant to the matters in question before its tribunals.

A.—As a rule there is no excuse for withholding evidence which is relevant to the matters in question before a tribunal, but questions tending to criminate, or to expose to a penalty or a forfeiture need not be answered.

Best, p. 174.

17. Q.—Under what circumstances can proof of former statements of a witness be given in evidence?

A.—Proof of former contradictory *written* or *oral* statements may be given in evidence, but before such contradictory proof can be given his attention must be called to those parts of the writing which are to be used for the purpose of so contradicting him; or the circumstances of the supposed statement, sufficient to designate the particular occasion, must be mentioned to the witness, and he must be asked whether or not he did make such statement.

R. S. O., c. 61, ss. 17 and 18.

Best, p. 804.

18. Q.—Where a creditor accepts partnership paper in payment of the separate debt of one partner, what presumption obtains in regard to the liability of the partnership firm?

A.—The unexplained fact that a partnership security has been received from one of the partners in discharge of a separate claim against himself is *a badge of fraud*, which it is incumbent on the party who so took the security to remove by showing, either that the partner from whom he received it acted under the authority of the rest, or at least that he himself had reason to believe so.

Smith's Mercantile Law, p. 41.

19. Q.—What difference is there as to necessities of presentation of a bill of exchange payable on demand, and a promissory note payable on demand ?

A.—A bill of exchange or cheque payable on demand must be presented the next day after the receipt in order to charge the indorser, but this is not necessary in regard to a promissory note payable on demand, and especially so if made payable with interest.

Byles, pp. 283 and 284.

20. Q.—In an action for foreclosure, upon payment by the defendant, what rights has he, in regard to documents in the hands of the plaintiff relating to the property in question ?

A.—Upon payment by the defendant, the plaintiff must deliver up all deeds and writings, in his custody or power relating thereto, upon oath ; and assign and convey to the defendant, or to whom he may appoint, free from all encumbrances done by him.

C. R. P., No. 187.

21. Q.—An infant hires a horse for riding but not for jumping, the owner refusing to hire it for the latter pur-

pose. The infant used it in jumping and the horse is thereby injured. Is the infant liable and why?

A.—The infant is not liable for wrong where the claim is in substance *ex contractu*, but he is liable for wrong apart from the contract.

In *Burnard* v. *Haggis, 14 C. B. N. S. 45*, the facts were the same, and it was held that using the horse in this manner, being a manner positively forbidden by the contract, was a mere trespass and independent tort, for which the defendant was therefore liable.

Pollock, pp. 144 and 145.

22. Q.—What is meant by a *novation*? Give an example.

A.—*Novation* is the substitution, with the creditors' consent, of a new debtor for an old one, as in the case of amalgamated Life Asssurance Companies under *35 and 36 Vict., c. 41, s. 7.*

A novation is not presumed.

Wharton's Law Lexicon, p. 510.

23. Q.—A. is in insolvent circumstances and negotiating with his creditors for a composition, which is opposed by B., one of his creditors. B., in consideration of the payment by C., a stranger, of a sum of money, secretly agrees to withdraw from opposition. Is this agreement binding and why?

A.—This is an agreement in fraud of creditors and is therefore void; and it makes no difference whether it was the debtor, or a stranger on his behalf, who paid the sum of money to B.

Pollock, p. 296.

24. Q.—Give examples of cases in which ignorance may afford an excuse for wrongful acts.

A.—In general ignorance is no excuse for wrongful acts. Exceptions : An officer of the Court, who has *quasi* judicial duties to perform, such as those of a trustee in bankruptcy, is not personally answerable for money paid by him under an excusable misapprehension of the law. Also an officer, who in a merely ministerial capacity executes a process apparently regular, and in some cases a person who pays money under compulsion of such process, not knowing the want of jurisdiction, is protected, as it is but reasonable that he should be.

Pollock, pp. 439-441.

25. Q.—Mention briefly the functions of Judge and jury respectively in the trial of jury cases.

A.—It is the function of the Judge to decide questions of law, and the function of the jury to decide questions of fact.

26. Q.—To what extent can a witness be compelled to answer questions tending to disgrace him ? Can his answer to such be contradicted, and why ?

A.—He must answer if the question is relevant to the issue in the cause. The doubt is when it relates to collateral matters, and is only put in order to test his credit. It seems indeed that in strictness the Court can compel a witness to answer under such circumstances, although in the exercise of its discretion it will not do so unless the ends of justice clearly require it. When such a question is asked and answered, the cross-examiner is in general bound by the answer so given, because the question goes only to the credit of the witness, which is a collateral matter, and to admit evidence to contradict him would be to raise a question not relevant to the issue.

Best, pp. 182-187.

27. Q.—Mention circumstances affecting the question on which of two litigant parties the burden of proof lies.

A.—The general rule is that the *onus probandi* lies on the party who asserts the affirmative. It is a fallacy of maxim that "a negative is incapable of proof." There is a distinction between negatives and negative averments determined by the affirmative in substance, not the affirmative in form. The burden of proof is shifted by *presumptions* and *prima facie* evidence. It lies on the party who has peculiar means of knowledge. Sometimes it is cast on parties by Statute. Wrong decision as to it is a ground for a new trial.

Best, pp. 371 *et seq.*

28. Q.—Point out fallacies arising from maxim "hearsay is not evidence.'

A.—This maxim conveys two erroneous notions to the mind: First of all, directly, that what a person has been heard to say is not receivable in evidence; and secondly, by implication, that whatever has been committed to writing, or rendered permanent by other means, is receivable. For examples see

Best. pp. 630 *et seq.*

29. Q.—What are the rights of a donee of a bill of exchange endorsed by donor in blank against the parties to the bill and why?

A.—The donor cannot recover the bill back or recover the amount from the prior parties; and the donee cannot sue the donor upon it ; but the other prior parties to the bill are liable to the donee.

Byles, p. 145.

30. Q.—Mention circumstances under which alteration in a material part of a bill of exchange will not vitiate it.

A.—Alterations in a material part of a bill of exchange will not vitiate it (*a*) when such an alteration is made before the bill is issued, or becomes an available instrument; (*b*) when the bill is altered to correct a mistake or supply an omission, and in furtherance of the original intention of the parties.

Byles, p. 337.

31. Q.—Under what circumstances can evidence of good character for veracity of a witness be given ?

A.—When general evidence of the bad character for veracity of a witness is given, then general evidence may be given of his good character for veracity to rebut it.

Best, pp. 363 and 808.

32. Q.—Compare the case of an instrument under seal operating in restraint of trade with the case of a promissory note in regard to consideration.

A.—In a contract in restraint of trade even though by deed, the consideration must be proven, but in a promissory note it is presumed to be for value unless it is proven to the contrary.

33. Q.—"Where difference of local laws in question the *lex loci contractus* prevails." Give exceptions to this rule.

A.—The *lex loci contractus* prevails (a) unless excluded by prohibitory municipal laws of the *forum*, (b) or unless the agreement is contrary to the common justice or interest of the state.

Pollock, pp. 388 and 389.

34. Q.—Define accurately, " *bill of exchange*, "*promissory note*," and " *cheque*."

A.—A *bill of exchange* is an unconditional order in writing addressed by one person to another, signed by the person giving it, requiring the person to whom it is addressed, to pay on demand ; or at a fixed or determinable future time; a sum certain in money to ; or to the order of, a specified person or to bearer.

A *promissory note*, or, as it is frequently called, a note of hand, is an unconditional promise in writing, made by one person to another, signed by the maker, to pay on demand, or at a fixed, determinable future time, a sum certain in money to, or to the order of, a specified person, or to bearer.

A *cheque* is a bill of exchange drawn on a banker payable on demand ; and is consequently subject in general to the rules which regulate the rights and liabilities of parties to bills of exchange.

Byles, pp. 1, 6 and 16.

35. Q.—One of three joint makers of a note is sued alone on the note. What course should he pursue in such action?

A.—He may give notice to the other two makers of the note and make them parties to the action; or he may sue them afterwards for contribution.

36. Q.—The principal creditor brings an action against the surety on the bond of suretyship without joining the principal debtor. What are the rights of the surety in that action (1) as against the principal creditor? (2) as against the principal debtor?

A.—(1) The surety may, as against the principal creditor, avail himself of any defence, which the principal debtor has against the creditor, and he may also set up any negligence of the creditor in loosing securities, or acting in any way prejudicially to the surety, and he also has a right to the assignment of any securities the creditor may have.

(2) As against the principal debtor, the surety can serve notice on him and bring him in as a party to the action, or he can sue him afterwards for the debt.

37. Q.—A contract between A. and B. to do something for the benefit of C. What right has C. to enforce the contract? Authority for your answer.

A.—No third person can become entitled by the contract itself to demand the performance of any duty under the contract. An exception is the case of marriage settlements.

> *Simpson* v. *Brown, 68 N. Y. 355.*
> Pollock, pp. 256 *et seq.*

38. Q.—How far is it an answer to an action to rescind a contract for the sale of goods to say that the plaintiff had the means of making inquiries?

A.—When the thing was actually *in esse* and the parties could have inspected, then the maxim "*caveat emptor*" applies, unless the vendor was the manufacturer of the goods or the grower of the article. It is no defence to the action to say that the plaintiff had the means of making enquiries, for, if any fraudulent statements were made by the vendor, he could not say the purchaser was guilty of any negligence in not making enquiries concerning them.

39. Q.—How far can the legal effect of a contract be altered or explained by the subsequent conduct of the parties?

A.—The subsequent conduct of the parties has no effect on the contract, if it is clear and unambiguous; but, if it is capable of two constructions, then the subsequent conduct of the parties may show in what sense the parties understood it and such meaning would be given effect to in the interpretation of the contract.

40. Q.—A. and B. are jointly liable on a promissory note to C. C. wishes to collect out of B. alone first, without prejudicing his rights as to A. Can he do so?

A.—If C. does not join A. as well as B. in the action he will lose his right against A. for they are jointly liable. He should sue them both and recover judgment, and then issue execution against B. alone, if he wishes to recover from him first, and without prejudicing his rights as to A.

41. Q.—What is the effect of an action where there has been a change of ownership *pendente lite*? What steps may the plaintiff take in order to preserve his rights fully?

A.—This has no effect on the action by

C. R. P., No. 620.

And the plaintiff, may, under such circumstances, add the new owner, by *præcipe*, as a defendant in the action by

C. R. P., No. 622.

42. Q.—What classes of documents are privileged from production?

A.--A party will not be compelled to produce documents if the disclosure of them might subject him to incrimination, penalty, or forfeiture. So a party will not be required to produce the muniments of title to his estate, nor will his attorney to whose care they have been entrusted, and in either case independent secondary evidence of their contents may be given.

Best, p. 301.

43. Q.—How does payment into Court by defendant affect the question of the costs of the action?

A.—If the payment into Court is sufficient to satisfy the amount found due to the plaintiff the costs of the action after payment will be allowed to the defendant.

44. Q.—A counsel asks a witness : " You say now that you were not present when the thing happened. Did you not tell S. that you were present then "? Witness denies that he did tell S. so. Counsel proposes to call evidence that witness did tell S. so. Is the latter evidence admissible?

A.—If a witness upon cross-examination as to a former statement made by him relative to the subject-matter of the cause, and inconsistent with his present testimony, does not distinctly admit that he did make such statement, proof may be given that he did in fact make it ; but before such proof can be given, the circumstances of the supposed statement, sufficient to designate the particular occasion, must be mentioned to the witness, and he must be asked whether or not he did make such statement.

R. S. O., c. 61, s. 18.

45. Q.—A. orders 300 pieces of calico from a London house on terms, paying for goods if approved at 50 days from delivery. By the time the goods have arrived A. has assigned to an assignee for the benefit of his creditors. The goods are placed in the Custom House and the assignee is notified of the fact. Before he takes out the goods a representative of the English firm claims them. The sheriff also sends down a bailiff to claim them for an execution creditor of A. Which of the three claimants is entitled and why?

A.—The London house has a right to the goods, because they never were accepted by A., and nothing was done either by A. or his assignee to reduce them into possession, and therefore the vendor's right to *stoppage in transitu* still existed.

46. Q.—A., being the owner of a matched pair of bay mares, offers to sell the pair to B. for $2,000 and gives him until 12 o'clock of the next day to accept. C. comes in the same day and offers $2,400, which A. accepts. B., hearing of C.'s dealing before 12 o'clock next day, comes and tenders to A. $2,000 and claims the pair. A. says they are sold to C. What remedy has B.? Why?

A.—B. has no remedy, for there was no consideration for A.'s promise to give B. until 12 o'clock of the next day to accept.

This was decided in *Dickinson* v. *Dodds* (C.A.), 2 Ch. D. 463.

Pollock, pp. 99 and 100.

47. Q.—A. has a liqudated demand against B., which is barred by the Statute of Limitations. He holds, as security, an assignment of B.'s interest in a property, which accrues

after the expiration of the 6 years. B. calls upon A. for a release of this assignment on the ground that A. has lost his right. How far can B. succeed?

A.—Lord Mansfield said :—"The Statute of Limitations does not destroy the debt but only takes away the remedy. The objection lies in the mouth of the debtor but not in the mouths of third persons." A lien may be enforced, where no action for its amount would be barred by the Statute. Hence in this case B. could not succeed in his demand, and A. would be entitled to enforce his lien against B.'s interest in the property.

Byles, pp. 355 and 356.

48. Q.—What proceedings can judgment creditors take to obtain information on oath as to the financial position of the judgment debtor?

A.—They may examine the judgment debtor on oath as to his financial position after execution has been returned *nulla bona*. In order to compel the debtor's attendance they must take out an appointment before a special examiner and serve a copy of the appointment and a subpœna on the debtor, and must also pay him conduct money.

49. Q.—How far does part performance of an obligation extinguish such obligation?

A.—Part performance of an obligation shall be held to extinguish the obligation, either before or after a breach thereof, when expressly accepted by the creditor in satisfaction, or rendered in pursuance of an agreement for that purpose, though without any new consideration

R. S. O., c. 44, s. 53, s-s. 7.

50. Q.—A. on the 10th of October, 1886, makes a general assignment to C. for benefit of creditors. On the 5th of October previously B. had obtained judgment against A. and on the same day had placed writs of execution in the sheriff's hands. The sheriff seizes the defendant's goods on the 9th of October, and then C. claims them. Who holds the priority?

A.—B. has a priority for his costs, but, when they are paid, then the sheriff must give up the goods to C. the assignee.

51. Q.—A. plaintiff, and B. defendant. Action to be tried without a jury. Both parties give notice of trial, A. for the Chancery Sittings, and B. for the Assizes. Where must the trial take place?

A.—The trial must take place at the Chancery Sittings for the plaintiff has the preference as to notice of trial.

52. Q.—What powers has the Judge in the case when at the trial a witness after being excluded returns to the Court without leave?

A.—The witness may be punished as for his contempt; but, though the disobedience will be matter of remark for the jury, the Judge has no right to reject his testimony.

Harris, p. 405.

53. Q.—Distinguish a *special* from a *general verdict*.

A.—*General verdict*, i.e., guilty or not guilty for the plaintiff or for the defendant—such a verdict being manifestly compounded of the facts and the law as applicable to them. But although the jury have always a right to find a verdict in this form, yet, if they feel any doubt about the law, or distrust their own powers of applying it, they may find the facts *specially* and leave the Court to pronounce judgment according to law on the whole matter.

Best, pp. 105 and 106.

54. Q.—What is the rule as stated by Pollock as to the effect of a contract made by a man when drunk?

A.—Pollock, C.B., put the ground of the liability as follows:—"A contract may be implied by law in many cases even where the party protested against any contract. The law says he did contract because he ought to have done so. On that ground the creditor may recover against him when sober, for necessaries supplied to him when drunk." But a contract entered into by a person who is so drunk as not to know what he is doing, is voidable only and not void, and may therefore be ratified by him when he becomes sober.

55. Q.—How far is acceptance necessary to a promise made by deed?

A.—Acceptance is necessary to a promise made by deed, although assent on the part of the grantee will be implied.

(N. B.—There have been excluded from this collection forty-three questions which have been repeated either here or in the previous chapters.—F. L. W.)

CHAPTER VIII.

EQUITY.

1. Q.—What is meant by " mistake" in equity, and distinguish between the application of the equitable rules : (1) As to mistakes in matters of fact, (2) as to mistakes in matters of law.

A.—*Mistake* is some unintentional act or omission arising from ignorance or surprise.

(1) *Mistakes of fact* are relievable with these important qualifications :—(a) The fact must be material. (b) The fact must be such as the party could not get knowledge of by diligent enquiry. (c) The party having knowledge must have been under an obligation to discover the fact. (d) Where the means of information are equally open to both, and no confidence reposed, there is no relief.

Mistakes of law as a general rule are not relievable— *Ignorantia legis neminem excusat.* But, (a) where a party acts under ignorance of a plain and well-known principle of law, and (b) where there is surprise combined with mistake of law, the Courts of Equity will grant relief.

Snell, pp. 522-528.

2. Q.—A debtor assigns certain of his chattels to a trustee for payment of creditors generally, and assigns certain others of his chattels to a particular creditor to secure a past indebtedness due to that creditor. What right if any has the debtor as to revocation of these assignments ?

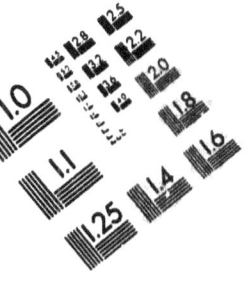

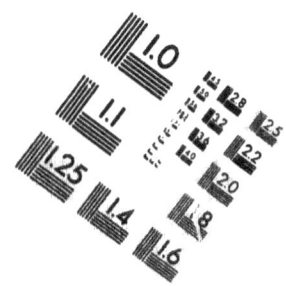

**IMAGE EVALUATION
TEST TARGET (MT-3)**

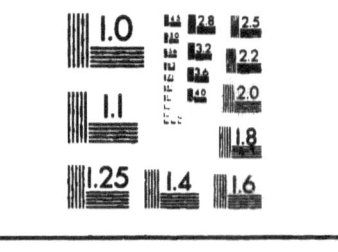

6"

Photographic
Sciences
Corporation

23 WEST MAIN STREET
WEBSTER, N.Y. 14580
(716) 872-4503

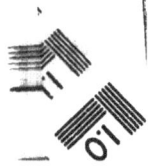

A.—Trusts in favour of creditors are revocable as a general rule ; it amounts to a mere direction to trustees as to the mode of disposition, and is an agreement for the debtor's own benefit and convenience. If, however, the creditor has been told about it, and he has in consequence been induced to a forbearance, it is not revocable. Where, as in this case, a creditor is party to the assignment it is irrevocable.

Snell, pp. 88 *et seq.*

3. Q.—A solicitor conducts a case until he has obtained a verdict for his client, and then procures from his client an assignment of the verdict, and a mortgage upon certain lands of the client, which assignment and mortgage were given to secure the solicitor's costs of the cause, including both those already incurred and those to be incurred. To what extent if at all can the solicitor enforce these securities ?   Give reasons.

A.—Any agreement between a solicitor and client, that a gross sum shall be paid for costs for business already done, is valid, provided the agreement be in writing. But in this case it behoves the solicitor to use great caution, and to preserve sufficient evidence that it was a fair transaction, and that his client was not under the influence of the pressure arising from the   relation of solicitor and client.

An agreement by a solicitor to receive a fixed sum for costs for future business was formerly invalid, and would have been set aside even after payment under the agreement; but under 33-34 Vict., c. 28, s. 4 (as regards contentious business), and also under 44-45 Vict., c. 44, s. 8, (as regards non-contentious business), a solicitor may contract with his client as to his remuneration for future services, but every such contract is subject to taxation as a bill of costs, and may (if improper) be set aside.

Snell, pp. 564 and 565.

4. Q.—A. is mortgagee of a property which is subject to a prior mortgage containing a power of sale. The prior mortgagee offers the property for sale, and A. purchases the same under the said power. The owner of the *equity of redemption* brings action to redeem. A., who defends, claims to have an *absolute title* to the property. Who should succeed in the action, and why?

A.—A. should succeed in the action, for he has an absolute title to the property, and is under no fiduciary relation whatever to the owner of the equity of redemption.

5. Q.—A., who is a married man, purchases the equity of redemption in certain real estate, which he then conveys to B., a married man. The land in question is then sold to C., a married man, at a tax sale, and is afterwards sold under an execution against C. The wives of A., B. and C., after the death of their respective husbands, claimed to be entitled to dower in the said lands. What are their respective rights in that respect?

A.—C. obtained an absolute title to the property at the tax sale, and the wives of A. and B. were in any event barred, since their husbands only owned equitable estates; but the sale under execution against C. does not affect the claims by C.'s wife to her dower in the property.

Armour, p. 145.

6. Q.—Explain the meaning of the terms "*surcharge*" and "*falsify*" as used with reference to taking an account in equity.

Q.A.—12

A.—The showing an omission, for which credit ought to be given, is a *surcharge* ; the proving an item to be wrongly inserted is a *falsification*.   The *onus probandi* is always on the party having liberty to surcharge and falsify.

Snell, pp. 190 and 611.

7. Q.—A. is the owner of Blackacre and Whiteacre, but each of these properties is subject to an execution against it, obtained at the suit of B.   Subsequently A. sells Blackacre to C. for valuable consideration, and gives a covenant against encumbrances ; and then D. recovers judgment and execution against A.'s lands, and places the execution in the sheriff's hands.   D. then brings his action against B. and C., to compel B. to throw his whole claim primarily upon Blackacre, in order that D. may recover his claim from Whiteacre.   What are the rights of the parties ?

A.—Marshalling will not be enforced to the prejudice of a third party, and, therefore, if D. could call on B. to have recourse to Blackacre, this would operate to the prejudice of C., who was the purchaser of Blackacre.   D. cannot succeed in his action.

Snell, p. 341.

8. Q.—A. leases a house to B., who sub-leases it to C., whereupon B. becomes insolvent.   Will equity afford A. any, and if so what, remedy, for the recovery of his rent ?

A.—Equity will make an order that C., the sub-lessee, do pay his rent to A., even although there is no privity between them, and A. will be allowed to collect his rent by distraining or otherwise.

9. Q.—A creditor recovers judgment and execution against one of two partners in respect of his own private

debt. The execution debtor has no assets except his interest in the partnership. What right does a purchaser at the sheriff's sale under the said execution acquire, and how can he realize upon his purchase?

A.—The purchaser at the sheriff's sale acquires all the interest of the partner, whose interest was sold, and he will be entitled to have an account taken in order to ascertain the value and have a division of such interest.

10. Q.—The executor of a mortgagee purchases the mortgage with his own monies for an amount less than that due upon the mortgage. For what sum will a person interested in the equity of redemption be entitled to redeem? Give reason for your answ'

A.—If trustees or executors buy up any debt or encumbrance, *to which the trust estate is liable*, for a less sum than is actually due thereon, they will not be allowed to take the benefit to themselves; but the creditors, or legatees, or other *cestui que trust* shall have the advantage of it.

Snell, p. 160.

In this question, if the purchase of the mortgage by the executor was *bona fide*, then the executor has a right to claim the full value of the mortgage; and any one outside, as the mortgagor or a stranger interested in the equity of redemption, would have to pay the full clair 'n order to redeem. However, the executor may have to account to the estate.

11. Q.—The Courts in this Province allow trustees to avail themselves of the provisions of the Imperial Trustees Relief Act (10-11 Vict., c. 86), and amending acts, as to payment of trust funds into Court. Whence is their jurisdiction for that purpose derived?

A.—In the case of an assignment of a debt or other chose
in action, if the debtor, trustee, or other person liable in
respect of the debt or chose in action, shall have had notice
that such assignment is disputed by the assignor or any
one claiming under him, or of any other opposing or con-
flicting claims to such debt or chose in action, he shall be
entitled, if he think fit, to call upon the several persons
making c'aim thereto to interplead concerning the same,
or he may, if he think fit, pay the same into the High
Court under and in conformity with the provisions of law
for the relief of trustees.

R. S. O., c. 44, s. 53, s-s. 5.

12. Q.—A. and B. enter into a contract in this Province
whereby A. agrees to sell to B. certain lands in Manitoba.
A. subsequently refuses to perform his part of the contract.
Can B. maintain an action for specific performance in the
Courts of this Province? Give reasons for your answer.

A.—Yes, B. can maintain an action for specific performance of the contract in the Courts of this Province. *Ex
parte Pollard, 1 Mont. & Ch. 239.* "*Equity acts in personam.*" In the case of *Penn v. Lord Baltimore, 1 Ves.
444*, which was a suit regarding land in the United States,
Lord Chancellor Hardwick stated (in effect) as follows:—

"The strict primary decree in this court, as a court of
equity, is *in personam*; and although this court cannot (in
the case of lands situate without the jurisdiction of the
court) issue execution *in rem*, e.g., by elegit, still I can
enforce the judgment of the court which is *in personam* by
process *in personam*, e.g., by attachment of the person
when the person is within the jurisdiction, and also by se-
questration so far as there are goods or lands of the defend-

ant within the jurisdiction of the court, until the defendant do comply with the order or judgment of the court, *which is against himself the defendant personally, to do or cause to be done or to abstain from doing some act."*

Snell, pp. 44 and 45.

13. Q.—A. is surety to B. for payment of C.'s debt. The creditor obtains from the debtor a mortgage to collaterally secure the same debt. Can the surety in any way avail himself of the benefit of this mortgage?

A.—Yes; the surety is entitled to the benefit of any securities which the creditor has or which he may acquire, and, in case the surety is compelled to pay the debt, he is then entitled to an assignment of these securities. And, if the creditor gives up or losses any securities, the surety will be discharged to the extent of such securities

Snell, p. 589.

14. Q.—Give an example of a case in which a Court of Equity will entertain an action to *perpetuate testimony?*

A.—A Court of Equity will entertain an action to perpetuate testimony, if the party, who filed the bill, could not bring the matter into immediate judicial investigation (which might have happened when his title was in remainder),or if he himself was in actual possession of the property.

Snell, p. 720.

15. Q.—What broad distinction is there between common law liens and equitable liens upon personal property?

A.—In order to have a lien at common law, the person claiming it must have the possession of the property, but this is not necessary in equity.

Taylor, s. 1085.

16. Q.—What are the liabilities of a mortgagee in possession?

A.—He is liable for rents received, or which he ought to have received, and may be liable for occupation rent. He can only charge for necessary repairs, and shall not be permitted to charge for his own personal trouble, but he may have a receiver appointed to take the rents and profits. He is liable to account to the mortgagor and can only have principal, interest, and costs.

Snell, p. 366.

17. Q.—"Assets will not be marshalled by a Court of Equity in favor of a charity." Illustrate this proposition by an example.

A.—A testator gives real and personal estate to trustees upon trust to sell and pay his debts and legacies, and bequeaths the residue to charity. Equity will not marshal the assets by throwing the debts and ordinary legacies upon the proceeds of the real estate in order to leave the pure personalty for charity.

Snell, p. 124.

18. Q.—A testator gave a power to his executors to sell a certain parcel of the testator's land and appointed B. and C. his executors. B. died and C. sold the property to a purchaser, who objected to the title on the ground that C. had no power to convey. Was the objection well taken or otherwise?

A.—The objection was not well taken, for in the event of the death of one executor the survivor or survivors have full power.

19. Q.—Real estate is conveyed to trustees by a deed, which directs them to sell the property in ten years from the execution of the deed ; real estate is by a will devised to trustees upon trust to sell the same whenever it shall appear advantageous so to do. When does conversion take place in each case ?

A.—In the first case conversion takes place at the end of ten years from the execution of the deed. In the second case conversion takes place at the death of the testator.

Snell, p. 208.

20. Q.—A. is entitled under a will to a share in lands, which are by the will directed to be purchased by moneys thereby bequeathed, and to a share of the moneys to arise from lands, which are by the will directed to be sold. A. desires in each case to retain his share in the condition in which it is before conversion. What are his rights in this respect ?

A.—He will be allowed to take, in the first instance, the money which was directed to be spent in the purchase of lands ; but in the second instance, he will not be allowed to elect to take the land instead of the money, since, by so doing, the sale of the rest of the land might be prejudiced.

Taylor, s. 100.

21. Q.—What is the application of the doctrine of resulting trusts, to the case of a conveyance of land without consideration ?

A.—Formerly in a conveyance without consideration there was a resulting trust in favor of the grantor, but now by Statute there would be no resulting trust.

22. Q.—Is there any, and if so what, distinction with
regard to its effect, upon the validity of an award, between
a case where the arbitrators make a mistake of law appearing on the face of their award upon a material point, and
a case where they admit the law, and decide contrary
thereto for the purpose of doing what they deem to be
justice in the matter.

A.—In the first case the Court of Equity will grant relief
where it is plain there was a mistake of law or fact.

Taylor, s. 1203.

In the second case relief will not be granted, for arbitrators are not bound to award on mere dry principles of law.

Taylor, s. 1204.

23. Q.—Illustrate by example the application of the
maxim that "equity looks upon that as done which ought
to have been done."

A.—This maxim is well exemplified in the cases under
the head of conversion, as, when there is a direction in a
will to sell all the real estate, and, with the money thus
obtained, to pay off debts and legacies. Equity considers
the conversion to have taken place immediately after the
death of the testator, even though the lands be not sold for
a considerable time afterwards.

Snell, p. 48.

24. Q.—A. and B. enter into partnership for the purpose
of carrying on business as pickpockets in Toronto during
the Fall Exhibition, and they agree that the daily profits
of the business shall be deposited in a bank to the credit of
their joint account, and at the termination of the venture
shall be equally divided between them. At the proper

time the money in the bank is equally divided, but A. sub-sequently discovers that B. had from day to day concealed a portion of the said profits, and had failed to deposit them. By what legal process if any can A. recover his share as agreed upon ?

A.—He cannot recover anything because the partnership was illegal.

25. Q.—What steps must a simple contract creditor take in order to give him a status to maintain an action on his sole account to set aside a fraudulent conveyance made by his debtor ?

A.—He must enter an action and get judgment, for only judgment creditors can apply to set aside a fraudulent conveyance made by the debtor.

But it now appears that a simple contract creditor may sue as well on his own behalf as all other creditors, to recover the amount of his claim and set aside the fraudulent conveyance.

26. Q.—Give an example illustrating the rule at law, and the rule in equity, as to *time being the essence of the contract ?*

A.—In a contract for the sale of land with a date fixed for its completion, at common law time would be of the essence of the contract, but in equity it would be otherwise.

Snell, p. 355.

27. Q.—What relief will equity afford in case of (1) the non-execution of a power, (2) the non-execution of a trust, (3) the defective execution of a power, (4) the defective execution of a trust ?

A.—(1) The general rule is that the non-execution of a power will not be aided in equity, unless the power is coupled with a trust, but if it is (3) the defective execution of a power equity will relieve in favor of a (*a*) purchaser, (*b*) creditor, (*c*) wife, (*d*) child and (*e*) charity, where the defect is not of the essence of the power.

Snell, p. 514.

(2) As to the non-execution of a trust, *equity never wants for a trustee.*

Snell, p. 152.

(4) As to defective execution of trusts, equity will afford relief only where the trust is for value, and in case of a charity.

Snell, p. 118.

28. Q.—An executor recovers judgment against a supposed debtor to the estate which has been administered and enforces payment by execution and distributes the moneys among the creditors of the estate. Subsequently this judgment is reversed on appeal. State fully the rights of the parties to the transaction.

A.—The debtor can recover the money back from the executor, and the executor can recover it from the creditors. This comes under the head of accident, and is an exception to the general rule, which is that you can only recover from the creditors and not from the executor.

Taylor, s. 71.

29. Q.—A testator devises his farm to A. and bequeaths his personal property to B. After the testator's death, the farm is sold under an execution recovered by a creditor of the testator against the executor. Does A. take any benefit under the will or is his claim defeated by the execution sale ?

A.—A. is entitled to the value of the farm from the estate. The personalty is primarily liable for all debts, and, until that is exhausted, the realty should not be used for that purpose And the result would be the same since the Devolution of Estates Act.

30. Q.—A. is owner of a farm, and B. assumes to make a mortgage of the farm, which the mortgagee registers against the same. What relief, if any, can A. obtain in equity?

A.—Where a deed appears upon the register, made by a person who has no apparent title, the Courts have held that the owner of the land has a right to its cancellation.

Armour, p. 133.

31. Q.—Give examples showing where specific performance will be refused (1) for want of consideration, (2) for want of mutuality.

A.—(1) Specific performance will be refused where an agreement for the sale of land is without consideration.

(2) Specific performance will not be decreed when the contract is with an infant since there would be no mutuality between the parties to the contract.

32. Q.—Explain what is meant by the term *sui juris*.

A.—*Sui juris (L. of his own right.)* A person who is neither a minor, nor insane, nor subject to any other disability is said to be *sui juris*.

33. Q.—Speaking of specific performance it is said that Courts of Equity will let in the defendant to defend himself by evidence to resist a decree, when the plaintiff would not

always be permitted to establish his case by like evidence. Illustrate this passage by an example.

A.—This principle is well illustrated by the case of *Townsend* v. *Strangroom, 6 Ves. 328*, referred to by
Snell, pp. 649 and 650.

34. Q.—Lands are devised, under the will of A., to B. in trust to raise money on the security thereof, for the purpose of complying with certain directions in the will. B., in pursuance of the provisions of the will, mortgages the said lands by an instrument in which he is described as trustee under the will of A., and in which he enters into the ordinary mortgage covenants, as contained in the Short Forms Act. Default having been made in payment, the mortgagee seeks to recover payment of the mortgage money from B. personally. B. defends on the ground that, by his covenant, he intended to bind, and did bind, the trust estate only. Who should succeed ?

A.—B. is personally liable on the mortgage and should have taken the proper precaution at the time he made the mortgage if he wished to escape this liability.

35. Q.—The estate of a testator is sufficient to satisfy both debts and legacies and the executor pays all the debts and all the legacies, except one. All the legatees are entitled to rank *pari passu*. Subsequently the executor wastes all the balance of the estate, and thereupon the unsatisfied legatee seeks to procure payment by the other legatees of such ratable proportion as will enable him to share equally with them. What are the rights of the parties ?

A.—The legatee can recover against the executor, who is liable for waste, but he cannot have recourse against the other legatees.

36. Q.—A surety is sued. He delivers his defence, setting up that, the principal debtor having failed to pay the interest on the debt when it became due, it was afterwards agreed between the creditor and the principal debtor that, in consideration of the latter's then paying the interest theretofore due, the creditor would give him six months additional time to pay the debt. On demurrer to this defence for whom would you give judgment?

A.—Judgment should be given for the plaintiff. There was no consideration for the promise to give time and this, therefore, was not binding on the creditor ; he could have sued the debtor at any time, and the surety was in no way prejudiced.

37. Q.—A. purchased real estate and took the title in his own name, but B. p id the purchase money. B. sued A. for the conveyance of the title and A. pleaded the Statute of Frauds, to which B. demurred. Ought the demurrer to be sustained or overruled?

A.—The demurrer should be sustained, for A. had no right to the property. There was an implied trust in favor of B., the party who paid the purchase money, and he had a right to ask A. to convey the property.

38. Q.—Two physicians are in partnership. One of them is guilty of intentional maltreatment of a patient. Is the other partner liable to the patient?

A.—No, the other partner is not liable, for this was a criminal act, and had nothing to do with the partnership business.

39. Q.—A member of a law firm borrows money and gives the firm's note without the knowledge of the other member. Is the firm bound?

A.—No, the firm is not bound because this is not within the scope of the partnership business.

40. Q.—Define *injunction* and *mandamus*.

A.—An *injunction* is the discretionary process of prevention and remedial justice, whereby a person is required to refrain from doing a specified meditated wrong, not amounting to a crime.

A *mandamus* is a high prerogative writ of a most extensive remedial nature, and commands the doing of something therein named. It is used principally for public purposes, but sometimes, however, to enforce private rights.

Wharton's Law Lexicon, pp. 371 and 451.

41. Q.—When will executors who place money with bankers for deposit or investment be liable for loss?

A.—The executors will be liable, if directed by the will to invest otherwise, and have left a larger sum there on deposit than was necessary. And the executors must place the money to a separate account even when they are directed to invest by deposit.

42. Q.—When will a bequest to a creditor not amount to satisfaction of a debt?

A.—When it is less than the debt it is never satisfaction. When it is greater than the debt it may be satisfaction *pro tanto*. When it is exactly the same as the debt it will then be a satisfaction. If the debt is incurred after the will this will not amount to satisfaction, and, in all cases, equity will lay hold of the slightest circumstances to prevent satisfaction.

Snell, p. 274.

43. Q.—Explain and illustrate by an example the maxim "*in pari delicto portior est conditio possidentis*"?

A.—*In pari delicto portior est conditio possidentis.* Where both parties are equally in the wrong the defendant holds the stronger ground. The law will take hold of an illegal transaction to defeat a suit, not to maintain one.

44. Q.—A. according to the life tables has an expectation of two years life, and upon this basis he purchased for $10,000 from a life assurance company an annuity to be paid to him during the balance of ' :; life. On the following day he is run over by a railway train and killed. Can his representatives obtain any, and if so what relief against the insurance company?

A.—The representatives cannot get any relief. This is a positive contract and is not relievable on the ground of accident.

___

(N.B.—From this collection there have been excluded forty-seven questions, which were repeated either here or in the previous chapters.—F. L. W.

PART III.

LAW SOCIETY

EXAMINATION PAPERS

FOR

CERTIFICATE OF FITNESS AND
CALL TO THE BAR

BEFORE HILARY AND EASTER TERMS, 1890.

Q.A.—13

PART III.

EXAMINATION PAPERS.

EXAMINATION BEFORE HILARY TERM : 1890.

Examiner : P. H. Drayton.

CERTIFICATE OF FITNESS.

REAL PROPERTY.

1. Is it necessary that the witnesses to a will should sign their names in the presence of each other ?

2. In what manner may a trustee invest trust funds where there is no direction in the will to guide him ?

8. What is a vendor's lien ? In what way may it be defeated ?

3. State the four general principles to be observed in the construction of wills.

5. Distinguish between a *marketable* and a *doubtful* title.

6. A., a married man, owns two estates, Blackacre and Whiteacre. Blackacre is sold under an execution. Whiteacre for arrears of taxes. What effect has each sale upon the wife's rights to dower ?

7. A writ of *fi. fa.* lands of a vendor is placed in the hands of the sheriff after delivery, but before registration of the deed. Does it bind the lands in the hands of the purchaser ? Explain.

8. To what covenants is a purchaser entitled on a purchase from a trustee ?

9. What effect has a registered *lis pendens* upon the title of a purchaser subsequent thereto ?

10. To what extent does constructive notice affect a *bona fide* purchaser under the Registry Act of this Province ?

EXAMINATION BEFORE HILARY TERM : 1890.

Examiner: R. E. KINGSFORD.

CERTIFICATE OF FITNESS.

BENJAMIN—SMITH.

1. What are the three general grounds of *illegality* of contracts at common law ?

2. What is the effect, if any, as regards the Statute of Limitations of a written acknowledgment of a debt containing a promise to pay it upon a certain condition ?

3. Goods are sold in Montreal, to be delivered in Toronto. When delivered to the railway company in Montreal, they are in good order, but on the way become unavoidably deteriorated by the conveyance. Must the loss be borne by the vendor or vendee ? Why ?

4. What is the difference between a *lease* and an *agreement for a lease* as regards the necessity for a writing ?

5. A. sends by mail to B. an offer to sell him goods at a certain price, and the next day he mails a letter revoking the offer. B., after the mailing of the revocation, but before receiving it, mails a letter to A. accepting the offer. Is there any contract ? Why ?

6. How far does delivery of goods to a carrier go towards constituting an *acceptance* and *receipt* to satisfy the Statute of Frauds ?

7. A. sells to B. for $30 a stack of hay standing on A.'s farm. The hay is to remain where it is for three months, and is to be paid for before removal. Before the three months expire, and before removal, or payment, the hay is burnt without the fault of any one. Who bears the loss, and why?

8. Explain briefly the difference between a *condition precedent*, and a *warranty*.

9. Goods which have been sold remain in possession of the vendor. The vendee having made default in payment of the price, the vendor re-sells the goods. Is he liable to an action by the vendee? If so, in what way, and for what amount?

10. A. and B. enter into a written contract by which A. is to serve B. for six months at $20 per month. In an action by A. for his wages, will B. be permitted to give parol evidence to shew that a week after the written contract was made it was verbally agreed that in consideration of certain privileges to A. he was to receive only $15 per month instead of $20? Give reasons.

EXAMINATION BEFORE HILARY TERM : 1880.

Examiner : P. H. DRAYTON.

CERTIFICATE OF FITNESS.

EQUITY.

1. Are contracts entered into with lunatics void, or void-able only ?   Explain.

2. What are the provisions of the Act 27 Eliz., ch. 4 ? Are they in any way affected by Provincial Legislation, if so, how ?

3. A. believes himself to be the owner of a certain lot in Toronto, and on the faith of such belief proceeds to erect thereon a valuable building, it turns out on an action of ejectment brought by B., that he B., is the true owner. Can A. obtain any compensation ?   Give reasons for your answer.

4. A. and B. are respectively vendor and purchaser of a certain property. Acting for A. you serve certain requisitions on title on B.'s solicitor, which he says he is not bound to answer, and that the questions raised do not affect the title. What steps should you take to have the matter judicially decided ?

5. Under what circumstances will the giving of time by a creditor to the principal debtor discharge a surety and

when not ? Explain also the doctrine of contribution between co-sureties.

6. Distinguish between tacking and consolidation, and state how, if in any way, they have been affected by Provincial Legislation.

7. Where a right, title, or interest in lands is in question what step can a plaintiff take so as to prevent the land being conveyed to an innocent purchaser without notice of plaintiff's claim.

8. State some cases in which the Courts will order an account between partners without a view to the final dissolution of the partnership.

9. What are, and what are not, sufficient acts of part performance of a contract for the sale of lands to take a case out of the operation of the Statute of Frauds ? Give reasons for your answer.

10. Define, and illustrate by an example, the *cy-pres* doctrine.

EXAMINATION BEFORE HILARY TERM : 1890.

Examiner : R. E. KINGSFORD.

CERTIFICATE OF FITNESS.

MERCANTILE LAW—STATUTES—PRACTICE.

1. A. is agent for B., and as such effects a sale for B. by fraudulent misrepresentation at a high price. A. is subsequently compelled by the purchaser to refund the money. He is then sued by B. to recover the price. How far should B. succeed ? Why ?

2. What is a *Charter Party* ? What are its customary stipulations ?

3. A. is mortgagee of chattels under a chattel mortgage whereby the mortgage debt is to be paid on a certain day, and the mortgagor is to hold possession until default ? Before default the mortgagor deals fraudulently with the goods. What effect has this proceeding upon A.'s rights ? Why ?

4. A., a purchaser of goods from C., being unable to pay for them, transfers and delivers them to B. B. verbally promises C. to pay for these goods. C. sued B. for the goods, and B. sets up as a defence that the agreement should be in writing because it was a promise to answer for the debt of another. How far is the defence good ? Why ?

5. How far can a surety revoke a continued guarantee under seal where there is no reservation of such a power in the instrument? Is there any difference in the case of simple contracts of continuing guarantee?

6. Give examples of promises *implied in law.*

7. A. is a creditor of B., and as such holds valuable security. B. pays A. money, and in turn therefor A. gives up his security. B. immediately thereafter makes an assignment for the general benefit of creditors. The assignee sues A. for the money paid him by B. What test would be applied to the transaction, and what would be A.'s rights? Why?

8. What statutory provision is there by which an assignee for benefit of creditors can have a claimant who does not furnish particulars of claim barred?

9. On what material can you obtain an order for replevin?

10. When may relief by way of interpleader be granted, and on what points must the applicant satisfy the Court?

EXAMINATION BEFORE HILARY TERM : 1890.

Examiner : P. H. DRAYTON.

CALL.

REAL PROPERTY.

1. A., who is the owner of Blackacre, agrees verbally with B. to sell the same ; he writes his solicitor giving him particulars of the agreement with instructions to carry it out. A. writes B. that the title deeds of the property are at his solicitor's office, where they may be inspected. Nothing more is done.   A. subsequently repudiates the contract.   Can B. compel him to carry it out ?

2. What was the reason and the effect of the statute declaring that corporations should be deemed to be capable of taking and conveying land by deed of bargain and sale ?

3. A. dies intestate, leaving real estate, and infant children. B. is appointed administrator.   He enters into a contract with a client of yours for the sale to him of a portion of the same. Presuming the title in A. to be good, what formalities would you require to be carried out before accepting the title from the administrator ?

4. What recent statutory provision (if any) has been passed touching the husband's interest as tenant by the courtesy ?

5. A. registers an agreement by B. to sell him Whiteacre. Owing to outstanding encumbrances B. is unable to give possession, but on completion claims that A. is bound to pay interest from date of registration of agreement. How far is B. right? Why?

6. A., the owner of a valuable store in Toronto, in the course of negotiations with B. for its sale to him, states that the premises are let to a most desirable tenant. A contract is entered into, but before completion the tenant makes an assignment. B. refuses to carry out the contract, and A. brings an action for specific performance, which B. defends. Who should succeed? and why?

7. Distinguish between the right to vary a written agreement for the sale of lands by parol, and the right to rescind the same by parol.

8. A devise to A., and the heirs of her body, on condition that she marry and have issue, male, by B. Construe this?

9. State the general law regulating the position of the signature of a testator in his will.

10. A. dies intestate without lawful descendants, leaving real estate, and leaving a father and mother him surviving. To whom will the inheritance go? Reasons for your answer.

EXAMINATION BEFORE HILARY TERM : 1890.

Examiner : R. E. KINGSFORD.

CALL.

HARRIS—BROOM—BLACKSTONE.

1. Give an example of *constructive breaking* sufficient to constitute *burglary*.

2. Enumerate the cases in which an officer may lawfully kill a person charged with crime.

3. Explain how far the *animus* is regarded in cases of breach of contract, tort, and crime, respectively.

4. State the main rules for the construction of statutes independently of the Interpretation Acts.

5. What facts must be proved to establish a case of slander of title ?

6. On a trial of an alleged murderer, how far will evidence be admissible to prove that the prisoner on a former occasion attempted to murder the deceased ? Why ?

7. What was the common law rule as to the mode of trying accessories ? What is the present law ?

8. When a prisoner on a criminal trial gives general evidence of good character, how may such evidence be met by the Crown ?

9. How far is evidence of *prior convictions* admissible against a prisoner ? How is it tendered ?

10. What are the different species of bailments ? Briefly state the essential feature of each kind.

EXAMINATION BEFORE HILARY TERM: 1890.

Examiner: R. E. KINGSFORD.

CALL.

CONTRACTS—EVIDENCE—STATUTES.

1. A contract is stated to be void on grounds of "public policy." State the principles which are applied to a contract in order to ascertain whether or not the contract is void on that ground?

2. How far is evidence admissible to shew that the object of an alleged agreement was unlawful?

3. A. and B. are contracting parties. X. is the subject matter of a contract which is supposed by A. to exist, but which in truth does not exist, and is known by B. not to exist. What tests may be applied to this transaction in deciding upon its validity? *Pollock* ★ 447.

4. A. effects an insurance on the life of B. How far do false statements made by B. to the insurance company concerning his own health, but not known by A. to be false, affect the contract? *Pollock* ★ 530.

5. What are the requisites for a sufficient acknowledgment to take a debt out of the operation of the Statute of Limitations? *Pollock* ★ 601.

6. To what extent, and under what restrictions is for-bearance to sue a good consideration? *[illegible handwritten note]*

7. How far does seven years' absence furnish satisfactory presumption of death? *[illegible handwritten note]*

8. How far are the Judge's notes of a trial evidence of what took place there? Why?

9. In a private action for a public nuisance, what must the plaintiff prove? *[illegible handwritten note]*

10. On a contract of sale state the obligations of the buyer and seller respectively, and state the requisites of proof in an action (1) for not accepting goods; (2) for not delivering goods.

[illegible handwritten notes]

EXAMINATION BEFORE HILARY TERM : 1890.

Examiner : **P. H. DRAYTON.**

CALL.

EQUITY.

1. A., who is a broker in Toronto, owns some stock. B. a customer of his, wishes to make an investment. On the faith of A.'s statement, recommending the stock as that of a customer's, he purchases the same. On discovering the true state of affairs he brings an action to set aside the contract. Should he succeed? Reasons for your answer.

2. A. B. and C. are sureties to D., in the sum of $9,000. for the due performance of a contract by E., who fails to carry out his contract. A. is sued by D., and judgment given against him for $9,000. In the meantime C. has died. State A.'s rights as against his co-sureties. Reasons for your answer.

3. A., who is a farmer by occupation, purchases from B. 100 acres of land, which he goes to see personally. The chief inducement to purchase the property is the representation by B. that there is on it a valuable quarry, which is exposed, the stone of which is suitable for a certain purpose, and therefore valuable ; it turns out that the stone is quite unfitted for such purpose, and comparatively of little value. On this state of facts A. seeks to have contract rescinded. Give your opinion, with reasons whether he should succeed, or not.

4. A., a trustee with funds in his hands for investment, consults with his solicitor as to investing the same. The

≡M : 1890.

some stock. B.
tment. On the
stock as that of
discovering the
to set aside the
or your answer.

sum of $9,000.
B., who fails to
., and judgment
neantime C. has
reties. Reasons

irchases from B.
)ersonally. The
rty is the repre-
)le quarry, which
or a certain pur-
that the stone is
iratively of little
io have contract
ions whether he

i for investment,
the same. The

solicitor states that he knows of an investment on a farm of $5,000, and states as his opinion that the farm is worth $8,000, the investment is made, the interest is not paid, and, on proceedings being taken to realize, only $4,000 is made. State the position of the trustee, with reasons for your answer.

5. A., the wife of B., brings against him an action for alimony. At what stage of the proceedings can she obtain interim alimony? And how, if in any way, can B. avoid the costs of application for the same?

6. A., who has been for years a confirmed drunkard, enters, when sober, into a contract with B. for the sale of his farm to him. The price is not a good one, and A.'s friends advise him to bring an action to set the contract aside, which he does, raising, as a reason, that his intellect has become so impaired with drink that he was wanting in contractual power. Should he succeed? Reasons.

7. Distinguish between a mortgage and a pledge of personal property.

8. State fully the rights of a mortgagee to distrain upon the mortgaged premises for arrears of interest as against creditors.

9. A. grants a lease of certain lands to B., he afterwards mortgages them in fee to C. The interest becomes in default, and the property is sold under sale, proceedings of which B. had no notice. What is B.'s position as regards his rights under his lease?

10. Land is by will directed to be sold, and the proceeds divided between A. and B. Can A. elect to take his share in land? Reasons.

EXAMINATION BEFORE EASTER TERM: 1890.

Examiner: P. H. DRAYTON.

CERTIFICATE OF FITNESS.

REAL PROPERTY AND WILLS.

1. A bequest is made to the children of A., to be divided among them equally when they attain the age of twenty-one years. Some die before reaching twenty-one, others attain that age. How should the property be divided?

2. What rules govern where legacies are repeated (*a*) in one instrument, (*b*) in two instruments, viz., a will and a codicil?

3. Within what time must a will be registered? What is the effect of non-registration?

4. A bequest to "A. and his family." Construe this.

5. There are several persons tenants in common of certain lands, they mortgage the same. The mortgagee enters into and continues in possession for 10 years. During the ninth year of his possession he gives one only of the mortgagors an acknowledgment in writing of his title. Who is entitled to redeem. Supposing the case of several mortgagees in possession for 10 years, when in the ninth year one of them only gives an acknowledgment to the mortgagor, what effect has this? Reasons.

6. What are the provisions of the Vendors and Purchasers Act, in respect of summary applications to the High Court.

7. State the nature of a mechanic's lien. Within what time must it be registered, and what steps are necessary to keep it existing?

8. A. owns a lot in Toronto, on a portion of this he has built a house whose windows look into the vacant portion of the lot. A. grants the vacant lot without any reservations to B., he then sells the house to C. B. shortly after commences building so as to obstruct the lights of the adjunct house. C. seeks to prevent him by injunction. Can he succeed? Explain.

9. Is taking possession of property by a purchaser a waiver of title? Explain.

10. A. gets his solicitor to draw up a will when in Toronto; this he leaves with a friend and proceeds to Manitoba. When there he writes to his friend to burn the will, which is done. Is this a good revocation of the will? Explain.

EXAMINATION BEFORE EASTER TERM : 1890.

Examiner : R. E. KINGSFORD.

CERTIFICATE OF FITNESS.

CONTRACTS AND SALES.

1. Could the rights of a party under a contract be transferred by him to another at Common Law ?   If so, how ?

2. State the principal rules as to acceptance in performance of a contract.

3. What difference is there as to right of action by vendor against buyer where the property has or has not passed ?

4. What is the liability of a carrier for delivery to a fraudulent purchaser ?

5. What effect has a sale dependent on an act to be done by a third person ?

6. If goods are sold on credit what is the effect of the transaction on the vendor's lien ?   Why ?

Suppose the goods remain in the vendor's possession after the term for credit is expired, what is the effect ?

7. A. signs a contract with B. for a purchase of goods over $40. He signs the contract without qualification. B. seeks to give oral evidence that A. signed really as agent for C. Can he do so? Why?

8. Explain the following expressions: "F. O. B." "Say about" such a quantity. "Sale or Return."

9. In what case is a sale of things not yet in existence good?

10. On a sale of an ascertained chattel is there any, and if so, what warranty of title?

EXAMINATION BEFORE EASTER TERM : 1890.

Examiner : P. H. DRAYTON.

CERTIFICATE OF FITNESS.

EQUITY.

1. A. and B. are partners in a mercantile concern. C. recovers a judgment against B. for a separate debt due him by B. What are the rights of a purchaser at sheriff's sale of B.'s interest in the firm. Explain fully.

2. Is possession of a property notice as against a registered title, if so, why ? if not, why not ?

3. A bequest to the Rector of St. James' Church, Toronto, for such charitable purposes as he may think proper. Is this good ?

A testator leaves $5,000 to be invested for the poor of Toronto, naming B. his executor. B. dies during the testator's life, and no other executor is appointed. How can the fund be dealt with ?

4. An executor desires to administer his testator's estate and distribute the residue without coming into Court, how can he protect himself against the claims of creditors of which he has no notice ?

5. Will a Court of Equity in any, and if so, in what case, decree specific performance of an agreement to enter into a partnership ?

6. Distinguish between the duty of disclosure as to facts in cases of persons applying for policies of insurance, and those of creditors seeking to obtain a surety for the payment of a debt or performance of a contract.

7. What is a writ of arrest ? Under what circumstances will the same be granted in this Province.

8. Where in an agreement a penalty is inserted for nonperformance, can one of the parties elect to pay the penalty ; where the other insists on performance ? Explain.

9. In what way should a trustee having charge of trust funds act so as to provide against liability in the event of the failure of his bankers.

10. A., a resident of Toronto, dies there, letters of administration are taken out in Toronto, and A. having left property in New York State, ancillary letters are taken out there. What law governs as to the distribution of the assets there ? Suppose there be a residue as to the foreign property after all claims paid, how can such residue be dealt with ?

EXAMINATION BEFORE EASTER TERM : 1890.

Examiner : R. E. KINGSFORD.

CERTIFICATE OF FITNESS.

MERCANTILE LAW, STATUTES, PRACTICE.

1. A. leaves a sum of money with B. under such circumstances that it may fairly be presumed that B. has authority to use the money or not as he pleases. Distinguish the duties and liabilities of B. as he does or does not use the money.

2. A. agrees with B. to build B. a house. Before the building is finished, and during construction, the erections are burnt by accident. Who must bear the loss? Why?

3. A. pretends to be agent for C., and as such assumes to grant a lease of C.'s property to B. What damages ought B. to recover from A.?

4. From what losses is a carrier by water exempt at common law, and against what species of losses will not even the usual express exemptions in the carriage agreement except him?

5. A Bond is made to A., B. and C. jointly, to secure payment of $1,000 to C.; C. dies. Who could maintain an

action on the instrument at common law? Why? Is there any change now? If so, what?

6. State the present statutory provisions in Ontario as to compensation for injuries to workmen.

7. A. has a factory in which B., C. and D. are employees; A. agrees with B., C. and D. that, in addition to wages, they shall be severally entitled to a share of the profits; the concern fails, and it is sought to make B., C. and D. liable as partners for the liabilities. What is their real position? What authority?

8. A. is killed in a railway accident in May, 1889; no letters of administration are taken out for his estate, but in April, 1890, his widow issues a writ against the company for damages; the company objects that the administrator should sue, and that there being no administrator, the action is not rightly brought. Is the objection right? Why?

9. State fully the limitations to the rights of a factor to pledge the property of the real owner.

10. In what cases can you get a writ of execution by leave of the Court?

EXAMINATION BEFORE EASTER TERM: 1890.

Examiner: P. H. DRAYTON.

CALL.

REAL PROPERTY.

1. A solicitor for a purchaser serves a set of requisitions on vendor's solicitor, reserving to himself the right to make further and other requisitions. To what extent will this reservation hold good?

2. A. enters into a contract with B. for the sale to him of a property of which the description runs as follows in the agreement: "A lot in the City of Toronto, more particularly described in a certain mortgage to the Canada Permanent." A. afterwards refuses to carry out the agreement, relying on the Statute of Frauds as a defence. Should he succeed? Explain.

3. A. by his will bequeaths all his personal estate to B., except $10,000 Dominion stoc. which he bequeaths to C. C. dies during testator's lifetime, what becomes of the $10,000 bequest to C.? Reasons.

4. A. enters into a binding contract with B. for the sale to him of Blackacre free from all encumbrances. A.'s wife refuses to release her dower. Has the purchaser any remedy?

5. A bequest is made by a testator to his "relations," who would be entitled ?

6. It is unusual to provide in conditions of sale that if any requisitions be made which the vendor shall be unable or unwilling to remove he shall be at liberty to rescind the contract. State the true meaning of such a condition.

7. What are the provisions of the Mechanics' Lien Act as to workman's wages ?

8. Where there is a bequest to one person, and in case of his death to another, at what time in event of death, is the gift over construed to take effect ?

9. Write a short note on what constitutes a signing of an agreement so as to satisfy the 4th section of Statute of Frauds ?

10. A., by his will, makes an absolute gift of all his property to his wife, subject to the payment of debts and legacies; and further on in the will says, " it is my wish and desire that after my decease that my said wife shall make a will dividing the real and personal estate hereby devised and bequeathed to her, among my children in such manner as she shall deem just and equitable."

State the rights of the wife and children under such bequest.

EXAMINATION BEFORE EASTER TERM : 1890.

Examiner : R. E. KINGSFORD.

CALL.

HARRIS—BROWN—BLACKSTONE.

1. At what stage and on what grounds can a motion in arrest of judgment be made, and what is its effect if successful?

2. Give an example shewing under what circumstances the taking of a chattel against the will of the owner will be (a) justifiable, (b) a trespass, (c) larceny.

3. To what extent does intoxication afford a defence to a criminal charge?

4. What is the difference between a civil and a criminal proceeding for libel as regards the defence of the truth of the alleged libel being a good defence?

5. If a spark escaping from a locomotive engine sets fire to a house near the railway, is the company liable? If so, what must be proved to make it liable?

6. A gas company employs a contractor to lay down gas pipes in a street : by the contractor's negligence the street is obstructed and an accident occurs. Who is liable? Why?

7. How far does the object for which a statutory duty is created affect the right of action for violation of it ?

8. What difference is there between the rules regulating the right to subterranean water and those applicable to the enjoyment of streams and rivers above ground ?

9. What is the gist of the offence of conspiracy ?

10. Explain *allegiance*. " Once an Englishman always an Englishman." How far is this maxim now true as respects the allegiance due to the Crown ?

EXAMINATIONS BEFORE EASTER TERM : 1890.

Examiner : R. E. KINGSFORD.

CALL.

CONTRACTS—STATUTES—EVIDENCE.

1. "There is believed to be one positive exception in our law to the rule that the revocation of a proposal takes effect only when it is communicated to the other party." State the exception. How far is notice to the other party requisite?

2. "There are certain classes of cases in which it may be said that mistake, or at any rate ignorance, is the condition of acquiring legal or equitable rights." Explain this statement.

3. In what cases can an agent personally enforce contracts entered into by him on behalf of a principal?

4. A question arises on the true construction of an arbitration agreement, whether the subject matter of a particular dispute falls within the agreement. Who must decide this question? Explain.

5. A. covenants with B. to insure his (A.'s) life within a given time. Before the end of that time his health be-

comes so bad as to be uninsurable. What is the effect on his covenant?

6. A. sells goods to B., and desires B. to send for them. C. obtains the goods from A. by falsely representing himself as B.'s servant. How far would a sale by C. be valid against A.? Why?

7. How may the genuineness of a disputed writing be proved?

8. In civil actions how far is the evidence of a husband as to communications made to him by his wife admissible?

9. What is the test for determining whether a plaintiff and defendant are in *pari delicto?*

10. In an action for disturbance of support of land what damages may the plaintiff recover?

EXAMINATION BEFORE EASTER TERM : 1890.

Examiner : P. H. DRAYTON.

CALL.

EQUITY.

1. State the general principles which apart from statutory provisions, or any special provisions in the instrument creating the trust, govern Courts of Equity in determining whether or not a purchaser of land is bound to see to the application of the purchase money when buying from the trustee. Is there any statutory provision affecting the same? If so, what?

2. Under what circumstances would a tenant have been able to file a bill of interpleader against his landlord? Reasons.

3. A. is lessee of farm Blackacre. The lease contains a pre-emption clause under which A. can purchase the freehold by giving two months' notice before the term expires, and by tendering the sum agreed on. He gives the notice at the required time, but fails to pay the money. The lessor refuses to carry out the contract, and A., the lessee, brings an action for specific performance. Can he succeed? Explain.

4. Distinguish between the effect of conditions in restraint of marriage ; (1) where there is a bequest over in default

of condition complied with; (2) where there is no bequest over. A father bequeaths a legacy to his daughter to be paid to her at 21 years if she does not marry until that period. She marries at 20 years of age. Will she be entitled to legacy? Explain.

5. A. is the executor of B., he writes to a supposed debtor C. demanding payment of $1,000. C. pays the money, and A., the executor, distributes the same with other monies to the legatees under the will. C. subsequently discovers that he had previously paid the debt. Can he recover same from the executor, and if he can, has the executor any remedy. If so, what?

6. A. and B. are about to intermarry, a parol agreement is entered into between them that A., the intended husband, will settle certain property on his intended wife B. After marriage a settlement is executed in pursuance of such parol agreement. The husband being indebted at the time, and afterwards becoming insolvent, the creditors seek to have the settlement set aside. Should they succeed? Explain.

7. Distinguish between the relief granted in cases of defective executions of powers. (a) Where the same are created by private parties. (b) Where they are specially created by statute.

8. A., as executor of the estate of B., is liable as such to certain covenants contained in a lease made to B.—he is about to assign the lease to C.—what steps should he take in order to be able to proceed to distribute the personal estate of B. without any liability to himself? Reasons for answer.

Q.A.—15

9. A. and B. are joint obligors on a bond to C. The condition on the bond has been broken, and the right of C. to sue thereon become absolute. Before action brought B. dies. State C.'s rights, giving reason for your answer.

10. A Guarantee Company enter into bonds for the good conduct and honesty of A., a ledger keeper in the Bank of Toronto. Sometime after, and during the pendency of the bond, A. is promoted to the local management at Guelph. In such capacity he embezzles a considerable sum of money. The bank sues the Guarantee Company who defend the action. Who should succeed, and why?